MW01504649

3ε

IN BED WITH
THE EXOTIC ENEMY

Stories and Novella

Daniela Gioseffi

Avisson Press, Inc.
Greensboro

Copyright © 1997 by Daniela Gioseffi. All rights reserved. For information, contact Avisson Press Inc., P.O. Box 38816, Greensboro, North Carolina 27438 USA.

First Edition
Manufactured in the United States of America

Library of Congress Cataloging-in-Publication Data

Gioseffi, Daniela.
  In bed with the exotic enemy: stories and novella / Daniela Gioseffi.
  p. cm.
  ISBN 1-888105-17-8 (cloth)
  I. Title.
  PS3557.I54I5 1997
  813'.54--dc21   96-49337
                                                       CIP

ACKNOWLEDGEMENTS: The author gratefully acknowledges these anthologies, periodicals, editors, publishers, producers and playwrights: "Daffodil Dollars" was a winner of the PEN Syndicated Fiction Award in 1990 and was aired in a dramatic reading on the National Public Radio show "The Sound of Words." "Rosa in Television Land" appeared in *Literature: Reading & Reacting*, edited by Mandell Kirszner [Harcourt Brace Javanovich, 1996]; *Kaliedescope; Stories of the American Experience* [Oxford University Press, 1993]; *From the Margin to the Mainstream; Writings by Italian-Americans* [Purdue University Press, 1990]; "The Spit of Hate" and "The Music of Mirrors" appeared in *Prairie Schooner* and in *Fiction 1986*, Exile Press, Navato, California; "The Exotic Enemy" appeared in *Women on War: Global Voices for the Nuclear Age* [Touchstone, Simon & Schuster, 1988]. "Mrs. Prism's First Death," *Ms.*, Fall 1976; "The Music of Mirrors," "The Fat Lady and the Snake Charmer," *Oxford Magazine*, Miami University, Oxford, Ohio, Vol III.#1, Spring 1987. "The Capitulation," *The Friends' Seminary Review*, 1976. Poetic sections of these stories, in differing versions, have appeared in *The Paris Review, Fiction International, The Nation,* and *Antaeus*. "The Golden Daffodil Dwarf" in earlier play form was presented at The Cubiculo Theatre and Theatre at St. Clement's, Off-Broadway in New York City, 1977-79. "The Bleeding Mimosa" was adapted for the stage by Luciana Polney and produced at The Duplex Theatre, Sheridan Square, Manhattan in May, 1996.

CONTENTS

THE BLEEDING MIMOSA

As I would not be a slave, I would not be a master.
This expresses my idea of democracy. Whatever differs from
this, to the extent of the difference is no Democracy.
Abraham Lincoln

Tutti gli uomini sono di natura equalmente
liberi ed independenti. (All people
are by nature equally free and independent.)
Filippo Mazzei, American colonialist writer

"You piece of white trash!" He spat an enraged whisper.
"You got lots of nerve commin' down here to follow
upstart niggers around my town!" My head hit the brick
wall of the jail cell as the deputy sheriff pushed me to
the cot. The bruised and beaten blacks from our
Freedom Ride, huddled in pain in cells along the
moonlit corridor of bars, were the only others in the
jailhouse. The deputy–squat, thick and muscular–stood
over me like a dark shadow in the dingy cell. Panic
pounded in my skull as he unzipped his pants. I
understood that I wasn't to be a Rosa Luxemburg or a
Fanny Lou Hamer, but an unknown casualty. His hands
with their reddened knuckles unbuckled the belt
tightened under the girth of his big belly. I thought he
was about to beat me with his belt buckle as I'd seen a
law man do exactly that to a black demonstrator that
very morning.

I thought how my father at home in New Jersey
would have another heart attack when he recieved the
news of my beating. His anguished face–a ghost of
memory–appeared begging me to stay at home in New
Jersey. He wanted me to give up my internship as a
journalist at the Selma T.V. station. The Klan had

burned a cross on the lawn of the studio after I'd appeared, a white spokesperson enlisting Freedom Riders, on a black gospel show. Television was not integrated in the Deep South in 1961—but I'd dared to integrate Selma T.V. My father had called long distance that morning to beg me to come home, but I dreamed of being the next Lucretia Mott, Jane Adams, and Faye Emerson all rolled into one. At twenty one, I was too young to realize mortality.

Following Rosa Parks' example, we'd ridden that morning on the wrong end of a bus seething with summer heat and racial hatred. For many, it wasn't the first ride, but it was for me. Then with other demonstrators, I'd taken a drink at a water fountain marked with a sign "Colored" in Tepper's Department store on Selma's Main Street. All the demonstrators on our particular ride had been arrested, but me. Some thought I was allowed to go home because I was blond, blue-eyed and young, but my arrest came later in the evening—when I tried to climb the front steps of the house where I rented a room from an ancient Southern belle, Abigail Brennan.

Abigail Brennan was wrinkled like an albino prune and lived alone in her rambling Victorian house in the oldest residential section of Selma, not far from Main Street, but secluded by an acre of mimosas, magnolias and assorted pines burdened with Spanish moss. Abigail thought "coloreds", as African-Americans were called then, deserved better treatment than they'd been given after the Civil War. She sat in her porch rocker, stroking her old black cat, and sighing. "People aren't freed from slavery, if they're freed without a home or job then told to pull themselves up by their own bootstraps! Not if they've been sold every which way and have no families besides, plus had the pride beaten out of them, too! That's what Granny used to say to me, but I couldn't say that to my preacher down yonder at the church. He doesn't want no Coloreds in his church—unless they sit in the back to the side, keep quiet, and put money in the box. His Papa was worse! Wouldn't even let em in the door—even after their church burnt down." Old Abigail sighed and petted her cat sleeping in her lap.

Walking along the small town streets in the evening, plush with trees dripping Spanish moss; front porches squeaking with slow rhythms of rockers; hearing local residents, as you pass, drawl out a friendly "Nice evenin'! Ain't it?" —you'd never know the unrest the town was in. The "Sit-ins" at lunch counters and "The Freedom Riders," riding on the wrong ends of segregated busses. Non-violent actions for Civil Rights were often followed by raids and riots then.

Abigail was no help when I yelled for help. She was hard of hearing and didn't respond from her bedroom at the back of the house as the deputy, with his pistol drawn, whisked me away in his squad car, warning me to shut up or he'd shoot me for resisting arrest.

"No one'll be the wiser if I do. Ain't none of your big shot niggers around now to protect you!" he said. "Ain't no newspaper guys from the North, and no managers from that damned rebel T.V. station of yours to hold your hand now, girl!" He laughed with satisfaction.

Seeing no one but the mimosa trees in the dusky shadows of Abigail's veranda, I obeyed as he cuffed my wrists behind my back. The deputy was the only law around for miles. There were no police to call.

We were alone in his unmarked police car on the way to the jail. He reached over and squeezed my left breast hard. "You're real pretty for such a piece of nervy Northern trash. How come you don't wear lipstick and powder like nice Southern girls? You'd be prettier! Doesn't your Papa know enough to keep you at home? He must be the dumbest guinea going to let you come down here all alone to work. Maybe he's really an upstart Jew with an Italian name. I heared they's lots of Jews in Italy. I bet you ain't no virgin. Your folks is probably a couple of Commies like them Northern Jew lawyers who come down here tellin' us what to do. You big city Northern broads think you know what the world's made of better than we small town hicks down here? Think we're just a bunch of Alabama cotton pickers down here? You think you got the right to come down here and break our laws? Think you're gonna teach us how to live and who to live with, who to eat and drink and ride the busses with?"

"My father didn't want me to come down here. It's my own idea." I spoke, softly, remembering the non-violent tactics I'd learned. Don't anger your adversary with your defense. "I know Alabama's more your home than mine, but people are people. We all have the same feelings inside."

"Niggers ain't people, our preacher said. The Holy Bible says so! I got no reason to think they is. We don't need your Yankee gov'ment down here. Your Yankee Dog, General Sherman, burnt my great Grandaddy's Georgia plantation down to nothin', or I'd be a rich man today! You understand? Not a hard workin' 12 hour a day lawman. A bunch of your lousy nigger freed slaves grabbed Great Grandaddy's land from him—a wild pack of niggers led by a Northern carpetbagger took squatters' rights, after they chopped off his ole grey head and left it hangin' in the barn for the flies to eat. Be glad I ain't doin' that to you, 'stead of just taken a little pleasure in you. Far as we're concerned, we won The War Between the States. My ole Grandaddy who told me that story many times as I was growin' up don't even consider us as livin' under the same gov'ment as you damned Yankees. He keeps that Confederate flag wavin' every holiday. 'We ain't stopped fightin' yet,' he says; 'we won't never stop, neither!'

That's what I want you to tell your pals when you go home. We don't give a turd what your gov'ment in Washington says about *integratin'* nothin'. If shovin' mustard and ketchup up your noses at lunch counters don't scare you all home—if burnin' crosses and flying watermelons don't send you packin'—then maybe you need a stronger lesson to get it straight. 'Cause um gonna get it real hard and straight for you tonight, little nigger lovin' guinea. We've lynched a few Jews and guineas down here, too. We got a whole big bunch of them guineas all in one swoop in Lou'siana once not too many years ago! Ain't your daddy ever heard of that bit of history?"

"We're only doing what's human. Please try to understand, Sir." I attempted to disarm him, by using a respectful tone, but he burst out with a long laugh.

"Well, ain't you polite for a dumb gal? Let me tell you something. If a nigger comes into our court to be indicted and calls himself 'Mr.' and wears a nice suit and tie, We throw the book at him. But, if he calls himself, 'Boy' and comes from the cotton fields covered in sweat and wearing dirty overalls and don't hardly know how to talk, We give him two bucks and send him home to work. If you ain't got my meaning, yet, this night in jail is gonna be your last chance to learn your lesson! Hear?"

I was comforted by the words "night in jail"

which implied I'd be let go in the morning and decided
to continue answering mildly. "Yes, Sir, I hear you." I
said, gulping down terror as we rounded the corner that
led to the jailhouse. No one else in the Student
Nonviolent Coordinating Committee would know
where I was, or that I'd been arrested. Everyone would
think I was home asleep.

"Maybe you ain't heard how the Klan got your
pal Viola Liuzzo in the head? Didn't you hear what
happened to that guinea broad drivin' her load of
Northern nigger friends home from a nigger march?
You got no sense, girl? Didn't you know that was a
warnin' to folks like you to go home and stay there? I
thought you T.V. broadcasters git your news hot off the
wires! That burnin' cross left in front of your t.v. station
was final warnin'. Since you ain't packed up and headed
North, you need another lesson, girl." He laughed and
put his hand on my knees.

My skin grew goose bumps of fear. "I've had
my eye on you, but I gave you one more chance. Then
you went around drinkin' from nigger water fountains,
too. You should've gone home after that flyin'
watermelon hit your ankle on ole Abigail's porch last
week. Weren't you scared for that ole lady, if not for
yourself? You could git her kilt, too, you know. You
don't seem to know how to take a friendly warnin', so
you got what's comin' to you now. Trouble is you seem
a glutton for punishment. You might enjoy every minute
of it. I bet you will, too," he said pulling my skirt up
over my thigh, running his rough hand up my leg.
Laughing as I shrank away closer to the door, trying to
open it with my shoulder."

"Now, girl, you don't wanna fall out while the
cars goin' so fast, and break them pretty legs, do ya? If
an upstart girl like you wants to throw herself out my

vehicle as I'm bookin' her for disorderly conduct, there's nothin' the deputy can do about it, is there?" I went numb with panic at his words. He sped up and I watched the asphalt pavement fly by in the headlights of the car. My hands behind my back ached as the metal cuffs dug into my wrists. To stay upright in the front seat without falling into the windshield, as he sped along a bumpy backroad toward the jailhouse, was all I could manage.

Dusk gave way to night as we arrived. "All my deputies have gone home for dinner. I'm the only lawman workin' overtime tonight." The jailhouse stood at the edge of town in a clump of willows laden with Spanish moss.

"How come you ain't greasy like them Dagos who run Dino's pizza joint in Birmingham?" He smiled. "That I-talian food's bloody stuff. Ends up more on your shirt than in your mouth. You got a pretty saucy mouth? Like that Sinatra. He's got blue eyes like you, but 'least he minds his own business when it comes to niggers, 'cept for that Sammy Davis monkey I seen him with singin' on T.V. like a dancin' chimpanzee. That's where all of your kind belong, singin' on T.V. up North, mindin' your own business. Not down here messin' in what don't concern you. We don't want you Commie pigs down here in our country! Remember my words, girl; go home and stay there!" He whispered his last sentences in my ear, as if he were a lover in the moonlight.

"Lights out, you niggers! No free show!" He'd yelled before he'd shut out the lights and knocked me to the cot. He fell over me crushing me against the springs of the metal cot. I heard it shriek out louder than my shivering breath. Then fear froze in my throat. I was petrified of being beaten to death. I remembered what Fanny Lou Hammer had suffered in jail. Anything I tried to do or say might make him angrier and rougher.

I heard a black man's voice through the petitions of bars yell, "Coward! God will punish you for your hate. Leave that child alone."

"Hush up your mouth, before you get us all beat again or dead." I heard a woman's voice answer. "You can't save nothin' with your breath. Hush before you make him mad enough to kill us all', 'cludin' that child."

But the deputy wasn't listening to their words. He was indifferent to everything but his own hands grabbing at me and tearing my clothes away, his heavy body crushing and pounding me into the cot, opening me like a knife. I bled from my mouth where he pressed his hard tongue and bit down into me.

I bled from my torn center and have never stopped bleeding like I did yesterday when a woman said to me, at a women's rights march: "You white feminists have got to learn to let us African-Americans lead you." I think of how I followed Rosa Parks, twenty years ago, into an endless struggle. I think of when I was twenty-one and wanted to be a T.V. journalist for justice, and my mother said: "You're a stubborn girl who got what was coming to you. Stay with your own kind. You're just rebelling against your father and me—like a fool. You should've stayed home where you belonged." Now at nearly fifty, when I think of how I have no close black friends because the white hand I extend in friendship is suspect--of a lack of self-worth, or because "guineas" are stereotyped as racists or Mafiosi. When I think of these things, I still feel that sheriff's hate invading my body. I feel him coming into the center of me where I bleed, because I never did go back to Selma except in my nightmares.

I've never told anyone about that night in Selma. Not even my husband. I'm ashamed of what happened to me. When I have a squabble with him, the nightmares come again. I don't really trust him or anyone—except my daughter now twenty-one. She wants to go to El Salvador to help the struggle there. My husband thinks I should tell our daughter that he adopted her, that she should be grateful and stay home and go to graduate school, instead of going to Central America. She doesn't want to listen. She says she's going no matter what we say. Just like I said years ago...no matter what...

How can I stop her? I tell her that it's dangerous as hell and there will be no definite victory? I explain that truth on your side isn't enough? How can I keep her from harm without taking her courage away? How can I explain that her father's not her father, but a mean spirited vessel of hate that forced me into submission and sent me home to live with my dreams turned to nightmares?

On and on nightmares bleed into the global heat trap of greed and hate that I can't stop my daughter from living in. I can't tell her she comes from hate. I can't hold her back and I can't let her go away. I feel rage when Mayor Koch runs to Howard Beach to get blacks boycotting Pizza, when people forget that Lester, the leader of that attack, was an Englishman born and bred in South Africa. I can't explain why I feel fury when the news reports everything about the fool who murdered Hawkins, but doesn't say a word about the Italian woman who ran down two flights of stairs into the street, even when she'd heard gunfire, to kneel over Hawkins, to give him resuscitation, to order an ambulance to the scene. How she held his hand trying to comfort him as he died.

My mother and father never forgave me for leaving home and going down South. My father shined shoes to be an American. He swept up ashes and sold newspapers to send me to college. He never forgave me, not even when he was dying. My mother still thinks I should've been a movie star. "You were good looking enough to be a star!" she still says sadly. "Why don't you bleach your hair, get a permanent, lose some weight instead of sitting reading those books nobody reads. What's wrong with you? You're making your daughter crazy too, going to all those anti-nuclear demonstrations! Watch out she doesn't get in trouble, too."

...hot flashes in the night, premenopausal sweat of a mother who learned to love what wasn't wholly hers...what was planted in hate and blossomed into love, for a young blond, blue-eyed daughter who rides the New York subways at night with looks of hatred coming at her from nightshift workers who think she's the enemy—who don't stop to think who might be whose. Who don't understand that we're all beloved of mothers, or fathers, or should be, and our hearts of darkness hurt us all, all are grieving hate, all of every color grieve and suffer hate, the whole earth bleeding now like a mimosa blossom spinning lost in space.

DONATUCCIO GOES TO SCHOOL IN AMERICA

...since justice is indivisible, injustice
anywhere, is an effort to justice everywhere."
Martin Luther King

If the arrangement of society is bad and a small number of
people have power over the majority and oppress it, every
victory over nature will inevitably serve only to increase that
power and that oppression.
Aldous Huxley

"Catch him! The little gimp's about to drown!" The sailor yelled as he pulled me back from the rail. I gaped down at the rushing water which had almost swallowed me. I wasn't quite nine years old. I'd tied a string to a tin cup and lowered it over the side to pull the mysterious sea up to me. I tasted it and lowered the cup again to see if all the big Atlantic was as salty. As the huge ship lurched again, a sailor grabbed me away from the edge of the deck.

"*Cristo, Donatuccio!*" My mother ran to me and hugged me. Then she shook me and wept: "I told you to stay out in the fresh air so you won't catch the fever! I'm watching your sister die in the stinking hold they call a hospital! *Gesu*, must you drown yourself? *Dio mio*, There's no place on this ship children are safe!" My mother was shy, but she wept wildly to the sailor who rescued me. She wanted him to know she wasn't a neglectful mother. He didn't understand a word of her Neapolitan. He smirked the way men smile at women. She was a Neapolitan beauty. She had a good figure—small waist and a big bosom. Her smooth olive skin, dark hair and black irises glistened in the sun. I was fair, blond and blue-eyed, like my father, Galileo, who waited for us to arrive in America, having sent us the passage. He was a Greek-Albanian-Italian from Apulia's Coast on the Adriatic Sea."*Grazie, molto grazie, Signore!*" My mother thanked the sailor of the U.S.S. Independent as she backed away, pulling me with her. She was always too humble and polite. Maybe she mistook the sailor's leer for *il mal occhio*, the evil eye. "May God always bless you for saving my son!" she muttered, crossing herself.

I heard the sailor repeat the word "gimp" as he walked away, laughing to his mate. I wondered about the sound. It was referred to me often on that ship.

My mother was small, only four-feet-ten. Unlike my father, I've always been short, too. She wiped my dirty face and looked in my eyes. "Your eyes are as blue as your Papa's! I'll die if anything happens to you, his first born *son*! There's not enough fresh water to wash the fever out of your sister." My mother held back tears. She had no one aboard that ship to talk with but me. My father, Galileo, had been absent in America for over two years. She was alone on that big ship. No brother, father, or husband to protect her. I could feel her fear.

"I was trying to get more water for Raffaella, Mama!" I held up my ingenious cup and string device. "I got the ocean in a cup, Mama, but it's too salty! I spit it out."

"Of course it's salty! It's the giant tearfilled eye of a miserable dragon!" She had many fanciful super-stitions. Lakes or oceans were the eyes of giant dragons bigger than we could see. I was always trying to find ways to help her with her work around the fields and cottage where we'd lived in Candela, a tiny village on the warm Apulian Coast across from Greece. From far off in the night, our mountain village looked like the flame of a big candle. In daylight, it's white stucco shone against blue sky. We were very homesick. The words "scarlet fever" had cut through the overcrowded steerage deck, a knife of worry. Our heads had become dizzy from rocking and our stomachs were perpetually upset. My sister lay feverish below deck.

"None of the other women will talk with me! They fear coming near the fever! Seven children have died since we left Napoli! Their ghosts walk the deck in the eyes of their grieving mothers." My mother was terrified. She'd lost four children in Italy. Two sons by miscarriage and twin girls to smallpox. While my sister lay quarantined below deck, she mumbled her frustrations at my absent father. "Why did Galileo make me marry him? No wonder my dear father cried at our wedding. He knew the grief Galileo would bring me—making me sail to America alone!" She wouldn't dare speak that way to his face.

The steamship company packed us aboard like sardines. I clung to my mother at night during frightening rainstorms at sea. She filled our imaginations with memories of home. "Remember how we jumped into the cool stream to wash our feet after a sunny day in the fields? Then we would walk to the village to fill our jugs at the fountain. I talked with the woman while you played with the town children! Promise me you'll play away from the railing, here by these portholes where I can find you. *Per favore, Donatuccio*?"

"*Si, Mama*!" I felt guilty for causing her more worry than she was already suffering over my sister. Before my sister became ill, we spent nights huddled together against my mother on the chilly deck. I wondered why a nice warm fire like the one in the

brazziere of our cottage couldn't be built in the middle
of that cold grey deck composed of a steel geometry I'd
never witnessed before that fateful voyage. My mother
held us close under her one blanket and told us stories
learned in her youth--Italian fairy tales like *Cinderella*,
Snow White, or *Pinocchio*. We loved to listen to her.

"Be a good boy and take care of your mother
while I'm away," my father had said to me before he left
for America. I was only six when he left and I could
barely remember him. If he didn't appear in America, I
decided I'd marry my mother when I grew up. What did
a small boy know?

"Galileo has kept his promise!" she had proudly
told the village women at the fountain. "We will soon
be leaving for America!" My father was an artisan who
thought the word "farmer" was an insult. His father,
Donato, for whom he named me, his first son, was an
important man in Candela. My father claimed that his
people had been in Italy before the Romans. Scholars
have now discovered that a third of the Albanian
language is ancient Etrurian.

"*Bambina mia*," my mother cried while
Raffaella died. I patted her head. I'd seen her bury two
shrouded babies in the village church yard. "Listen to
me, *figlio mio*. She always called me "my son" as if it
were a title. "Stay alive and get to America where Papa
says you'll have a better life. You'll be educated and
respected like your grandfather, Donato."

In the waters crossed by Columbus four
hundred years before, my sister Rapahella's small body
was slid from a ship's plank to its fathomless bed—food
for sharks. My mother cried out as it fell. I tightened my
grip on her hand. Even in my sorrow, I was glad to be
alive above deck. It was raining again as my sister slept
forever in the grey ocean, I watched its dark horizon.

The priest prayed in Latin to the sea, the sky, the cold deck. They didn't answer, except in the ocean's moan mixed with windswept wails of mourning women. Their rosaries hummed along with the murmured *Ave.* All but the priest and my mother kept their distance from the diseased corpse of my little sister. I tried hard to imagine I'd never see Raffaella again. The idea of "never" struck me profoundly. "Never," I thought. "*Non capisco nulla di niente!*"

We were so tired of being packed like sardines into the crowded rocking hold. Water was rationed among us steerage passengers. We had little to wash with and never enough to drink. The profiteering steamship company gave us nothing to eat that wasn't dried or salted. It was sickening! There'd been three days of fierce rainstorms—too cold to stay above deck. The Atlantic was so desolate; I longed to see the Goat Man of Candela again, to watch my mother smile at him. I wanted to run through the village streets, limping fast to keep up with the other children, my sister Raffaella with me. We were constantly cold and damp and unimaginably fatigued by our seemingly endless journey. At first, I'd been amazed by the giant ship. Now, I dreamt of it as a huge monster. It swallowed me, my sister, my mother into its bloody bowels.

On sunny afternoons in Italy, I would join my mother working in the green Apulian fields beneath blue Adriatic skies. We'd carry a few bartered vegetables home for our dinner. The tenant farmer for whom we worked took his share of the crops and handed the bulk to the landlord who held the yielding earth for his own family's profit. Foreign powers and feudal lords had pillaged Southern Italy for centuries. My favorite time of day was early in the morning. The funny grey goat, copper bell clanging the village awake, would climb the hill to our stucco cottage. Old Francisco, leading his goat by a straw rope, would stop at our open door. My mother would trade a small sack of hand-ground semolina for a bit of goat's milk. He always teased her as he milked, squirting his animal's teat directly into mine or my sister's mouth. Trying not to spill a precious drop, we'd laugh if he accidentally squirted a few on our cheeks. "The milk is clean and fresh as possible—direct from the breast!" he'd tell her. "Aren't you lonely, Lucia? When will your husband ever return from the Land of Gold?"

One day as my mother napped, I accidently wandered up off the steerage deck to a First Class area of the vessel. "Look Alfred, he's like the urchins we saw in the streets of Naples—how adorable!" An elegantly dressed, blond lady spoke to her mate in Italian—as if she were practicing the language. "Don't touch him, Alice. He's probably full of lice and disease! Her husband, stuttering over his halting Italian, warned her. "He's more like the urchins we saw in Rome, pale, thin, blue-eyed, like you. That's why you're so attracted. You read too many novels. Look, he's a gimp besides. They're dragging every sort of riff-raf into The States these days—cheap labor to undermine unionizing! No wonder the market flutters with these broken-down guineas, pollacks, kikes, chinamen they're dragging in. Come away!"

I've re-examined that moment many times over, perhaps because it was my first taste of Americans. I scurried back to my proper social position on the deck below, noting that once again that word *gimp* had been used with regard to me. I decided when I met my father again in America, I'd ask him what the strange sound meant--so like the one wild geese made as they waddled near our lagoon.

"You'd better do all you can to hide your son's lame leg." A wrinkled, white haired, Neapolitan woman dressed in black spoke to my mother in her own dialect. "My lame niece went through Ellis Island customs and was turned away—even after the doctor examined her and felt her breasts for a long time. You'd better cover your big breasts with a shawl and keep your son close to your skirts to disguise his limp. If they ask, tell them he sprained his ankle getting off the boat. Terrible things happen on *Isola della lacrime*."

"*Dio mio*, tell me about this crying island?"

"It's called Manhattan." The Neapolitan talked on mistaking which island my mother asked about. "The part where I live is called Mulberry Street—in `Little Italy,' but the only thing Italian about it is the people and bread. No blue skies, no green gardens, except in dirty patches by the toilets in the backs of *wooden* houses. Imagine! Junk wood that can burn—for us immigrants. My nephew builds stone and brick homes for the rich Americans on the Upper East Side, but we live in clapboards. I watch the *bambini* while my daughter bakes a room full of bread to sell every day. A widow like me is good for something until she croaks! Mulberry Street is so hot in summer, crowded with pushcarts, stinking with horse manure. We're packed like on this boat. What a stink below deck! I sleep in a corner under the pipes and pray for the rocking to stop. I tell myself, either you will puke up your bowels on this rotten ship, or you will croak on Mulberry Street. What's the difference?"

"But you won't die." My mother tried to reassure her.

"Don't be silly, child! We all die someday. Meantime, the bread smells good as it bakes and the children are beautiful to watch—like flowers blooming.

An old widow goes on as she must. I have sympathy for you—losing your daughter to the fever. Take the advice I give you. Carry your son close to your skirts and cover your breasts!"

"What? They hate breasts in America?" My mother was horrified.

"No, on the contrary. Men are men everywhere! My young niece was told to take off her blouse by the doctor who examined her on Ellis Island. Then he squeezed her all over for a long time, with a smile on his face. Imagine!"

"*Dio*! My mother looked heavenward and crossed herself. But, I won't be living on Mulberry Street. My husband is taking me to a city in the north. I can't read and he can't write. I don't remember the name of it."

"Schenectady, Mama!" I chimed in. I had a good memory and remembered the Italian telegraph messenger's words as he read to my mother.

"What a smart boy he is. He remembers everything. I'll jump in the ocean if they don't let him into America."

"Just stay calm and do as I tell you. Remember, people will be crushed in long lines in a big building. They put numbers on your back in chalk. If you have to go to the toilet, it's a long way and you lose your place in line. We'll stay together and mind our places for each other. You get so thirsty. It takes a long time for the examiners. They listen to the heart with things in their ears. If they don't like what the heart speaks, they send you home! They ask you to show your money. I'll hide mine in my shoe linings and only show them a little. Some of the officials tell you they will put it in the bank for you and then they keep it, or ask for it under the table to pass you through.

"*Gesu*!" My mother's eyes widened with horror. She prayed "Hail Mary" and bit her knuckles. "I have no money. My husband will meet us, he said."

"Just do as I say. I'll pray and light a candle that in America you will have healthy children to comfort your old age. You're so young. There's time. I know a woman on Mulberry Street whose children became so American they give her nothing. She has to work like an old dog in a factory while they live in the country. Imagine! She has only daughters and they married Irishmen. All her sons were lost in a factory fire!" The old Neapolitan seemed to comfort herself with tales of disaster, as if to say, "Look what we survive!" Like an Ancient Mariner, she captured my mother's ears. I fell asleep and dreamt of my disaster.

"My God, the baby fell from the table!" My aunt's voice had screamed. I was two, nearly three, when it happened. I was reaching for something and I fell from a high table. A fierce pain racked my hip joint. My father was away in America. There was no doctor in the village. When I got out of bed days later, my right leg was lame and shorter than my left. I'm like Humpty Dumpty, broken forever.

I stood, clinging to my mother, on the foredeck as we sailed through the Verezzano Narrows into New York Harbor. I felt hot and listless, but thrilled with a peculiar chill as we passed the collosal self-assurance of the Statue of Liberty. It's a cliche by now, but we were faint with the sights before us, tugs, barges, sloops, freighters, ocean liners busied the waters as we came into port. We steerage passengers gesticulated wildly, pointing at this and that in many dialects. "Mountains!" We shouted as the buildings of Manhattan came into view. In 1913 when we landed, Puccini's "Girl of the Golden West" was playing in opera houses all over

Europe. Italians were marvelling at American cowboy stories exported by Hollywood's silent movie boom. While my mother fought back tears of exhaustion, I was wide-eyed at every new sight before me. I felt hot as blazes and remembered Raffaella. "*Tutto passo,*" the old Neapolitan read my mother's grieving heart. She was one of those Southern Italians, fatalistic in the face of horror, used to suffering earthquakes, corrupt priests, pillaging invaders—for centuries.

The first and second class passengers went ahead. English speaking people had entré arranged for them by landed relatives and didn't have to go through Ellis Island—only we steerage passengers—carrying our ragged bundles, torn pillows, meager family heirlooms wrapped in scarves, sacks of household goods, whimpering with the realization of all that had been left behind and abandoned, *la via vecchia*, gone forever. But, Europe would soon be awash with the blood and suffering of World War I, so we escaped that, though we left blue skies for grey factories and tenements. First we waited on long anonymous lines and then were packed into rickety ferry boats and shipped to the customs hall of Ellis Island.

"There it is, *The Island of Tears*!" said the old Neapolitan. "*Caraggio*, you've come this far. She took my mother by the arm and led her. My mother followed her while half carrying me close to her long skirts. "I only want to prepare you for the worst, so you can rejoice in the best." Her wisdom served us well. We simply sat on our bundles and waited as others paced and strained to get a view of what was ahead. Years later, I saw a Chaplin film. A horde of swarthy immigrants, dressed in rags, having puked their guts out at sea, anxiously exits a big steamship in a frenzy to reach the shore only to be jerked back in their path by a chain pulled across their throats. It was like that.

"Keep moving! Hurry up! This way! That way!" Immigration Hall at Ellis Island was an old arsenal turned human warehouse. Officials barked in several languages, gesturing at us with our bulging parcels, wicker hampers, carpet bags, wooden crates dragged every which way. My father was no doubt lured by true stories as well as myths exported to Italy by the Land of Opportunity, but America played no fancy public relations game with us in that customs hall. We were shuffled along, weary imports of cheap labor: Italians, Jews, Poles, Catholics. "*Dagos* or *guineas*" we were called. Italians were sometimes lynched in the Southern United States, as late as the twenties. The largest lynching in U.S. history was of a group of Italians in 1891 in New Orleans. "*Lynch*" was the only American word that crossed the Atlantic and entered the Italian language of the time. No wonder my father chose a northern city of New York state. Yet, more Italians eventually ended up on the streets of New York than those of Rome.

The huge Immigration Hall was unimaginably crowded, a deafening Tower of Babel. We stood in lines and sat on wooden benches for hours and nearly died of thirst. At some point we were herded into a dining hall and given watery oatmeal with prunes on tin plates. As soon as we swallowed the tasteless slop, we were herded along lengthy lines between rope railings to be checked off on the manifests prepared by steamship captains. Numbers were chalked or pinned to our backs as we shuffled along a medical inspection line. My face was fiery hot. I held my mother's hand and buried my watery eyes in her sleeve. I could feel her anxiety in my lungs which refused to inhale deeply. As we came to our medical inspector, he must have seen my hair sticking to my forehead with sweat, my eyes dilated with feverish wonder. My face was red hot. He gestured for me to stick out my tongue. My mother swept me into her arms and began to explain in rapid dialect that I'd sprained my ankle leaving the ship. The medical inspector called an interpreter who fired questions in rapid succession at my dumbfounded mother.

"Tell her I think her son has Scarlet Fever," he must have finally said, as we were immediately sent to the hospital where we could better be examined for the dreaded contagion that had spread aboard The U.S.S. Independent. "Scarlet Fever! No question. You must be quarantined here with him." I heard the interpreter relay the official conclusion to my mother in Italian. I understood him well. I passed out on the cot where they placed me. When I woke a few minutes later, I listened in delirium as he questioned my mother: "What's your full name? Who's meeting you? Are you sponsored? What's your husband's name? Does he have a job? We will notify him with a pink slip when he arrives. He jotted my mother's answers on a form held by a clipboard. Even now, I can imagine him writing, but not his face, only his uniform. How old is the boy? How long has he been feverish? How many children do you have?"

"Only one still alive," my mother answered dejectedly.

My father often told the story of how he was pacing back and forth in the exit hall of Ellis Island. He scrutinized all the faces that came to the railing known as the "Kissing Post," because so many families had been reunited in front of it. Finally, he asked an official at the desk and was given a pink scrap of paper. An exhausted interpreter perfunctorily told him what it meant. "This says your daughter, Raffaella, died at sea from Scarlet Fever and your son, Donato, and wife, Lucia, are quarantined in the island hosptial. Come back in thirty days. If they've recovered you can take them home with you."

My father tried to absorb what he'd been told. He'd been dreaming for years of holding my mother again in his arms. He'd risen at dawn to take the first train from Schenectady to New York City. Knowing barely a word of English, he'd made his way through the labyrinths and bustling crowds of Grand Central Station to Battery Park and ferried to Ellis Island to meet us. He'd been planning the day of our arrival for months. He had a special dinner, which he could hardly afford, waiting for us at home. Now, in one sentence he was told that his daughter was dead and we were ill and might not recover. He had a passion for my mother and little else. He never mixed well socially in America and spent all his time working alone in his ghetto shoemaker shop on Strong Street—earning our passage so he could send for us. He returned home dejected and lonely, clinging to the slender hope that he'd see us again in thirty days.

"Aqua, figlio mio, agua!" My mother held vigil over me in the hospital, often whispering me awake with a cup of water held to my lips. She remained convinced that she could have saved my sister's life if only the steamship had allowed her more than her small ration of water when my sister fell ill. Each time I opened my eyes a cup of water met my lips and through my blurred vision, I saw Liberty's torch light glowing at night in my hospital window which opened on the harbor. "Water" and "drink" were the first two English words my mother learned. Her folk wisdom and loving manner saved me. When I started to mend, she sat beside me and told me over and over again, the story of

Pinocchio—adding many animated details to please me.
I liked it because my father, Galileo, was a shoemaker
and a craftsman, like Gepetto who carved Pinocchio and
made him lovingly into a real live boy.

"I won't be a fool like Pinocchio, Mama. I'll go
to school and learn."

"*Si, carissimo figlo mio*, just get well and you
will go to school in America," she whispered mopping
my forehead with a cool cloth. "At least there's enough
fresh water on this Island of Tears to wash the fever out
of you—not like on that horrible ship that killed my
Raffaella. Drink, rest, all will be well."

My mother slept in the stiff hospital chair
beside my cot, hardly leaving my side for a month. Her
back ached and she grew pale on Ellis Island. She must
have said a final goodbye to all her girlhood dreams and
invested all hope in my survival. I'll never forget my
father's happiness when he finally met us at the *Kissing
Post*. He swept us both into his arms and wept—despite
his manly stance. But, I saw grief in his eyes as he
watched me limp toward him. I could hardly stand after
a month in bed. When I recuperated, I felt twice as
sensitive to people's feelings—as if I could read their
unspoken thoughts.

"He'll get well and go to school. School here in
America will be good for him. He'll gain a profession
and his leg won't matter. The American public school
is free to everyone. It's not like the church school where
they steal your money and your children for the
monastery. He'll learn English and American ways and
teach us, too." My father encouraged my mother who
was weak and saddened by the voyage and Raffaella's
death. My recovery was her only hope.

I'll never forget the thrill of riding piggy back
clinging to my strong father's shoulders through the

bustling streets of New York to Grand Central station: the people, buildings, cars, commotion everywhere. Once we got to Schenectady, it didn't take long to realize that my father wasn't happy in his shoemaker shop. "Look at these cheap factory shoes they bring me to mend. No one asks me to make shoes from fine leather for them. They don't want my craft. Instead, I mend junk factory shoes for pennies. My apprenticeship—all wasted!" My father's craft had been replaced by the industrial revolution. Only a very occasional customer wanted a handcrafted pair of fine leather shoes. Then he would be happy while he made them. He fashioned for me a special shoe with the sole and heel a little taller in an attempt to correct my shortened leg. Working with my father around his shop, I was at last strong enough to attend school.

"No, *you* are not *me*! You are *me*. *I* am *me*, and you are *you!*" How can you not see?" The teacher scolded me on my first day in that strange classroom, and the American children laughed uproariously. I felt so foolish, standing with the teacher at the blackboard as she pointed to the words, "You" and "Me" which she'd written in chalk under the heading, "Pronouns." I'd never seen chalk before, let alone written words of any kind. The teacher kept pointing to herself and saying "me," and then pointing to me and saying, "you." But when I did exactly the same, pointed to her and said "me." And pointed to me and said "you," she became exasperated. All the children laughed and pointed at me. She gestured for me to return to my seat. With great relief and humiliation, I did. Everyone's eyes were on me and my strange clothes, ragged and homespun compared to theirs. The bell sounded for lunch and I sprang from my seat in imitation of the other children. They fetched lunch boxes and paper bags from their desks and ran into the fenced in yard of the red, brick building to eat lunch together. I took bread and cheese from my pocket and sat alone eating in a corner of the school yard.

One day, after I'd learned a little English, a boy called to me. "Hey, gimp, we want you to play ball with us!" Again, there was that sound the wild geese make in their throats. I didn't understand what he wanted of me, but I followed his gestures. I can still see his freckled face, topped with thick red hair, leering with glee at me. The school yard was paved with black macadam. The redhead showed me how to hit the ball with a stick when it was thrown. He gestured for me to try it. I nodded and stood before home plate, clutching the stick awkwardly, but if the American boy was going to be friendly enough to ask me to join the game with his friends, I wanted to do my best. After some haphazard swings, I hit the ball into the air.

"Hey, *guinea* gimp! You hit it," he shouted. "Now run, run!" I'd often watched them play. I ran as I'd seen them do—but limped awkwardly as I ran and the children taunted me. They crowded around me shouting, "Cork leg! Smelly *guinea*! What's that stuff around your neck?" The redhead shouted as he ripped from me the clove of garlic, a talisman I wore on a string around my neck under my shirt. It had bounced out of my shirt as I ran. "Phew! What a stink," he groaned, pretending to keel over, making the other children laugh at his antics.

A clove of garlic was worn around the neck to ward off *il mal occhio*. I was imbued with my mother's superstition and became terrified that I was now unprotected. I was learning for sure what the wild geese sound meant. I could see the derision in their faces, their "evil eye" as they shouted, "*guinea* gimp!" over and over. The redhead threw the garlic talisman over the fence holding his nose with a gesture of disgust. I fell over the rock which had been laid out as first base, trying to capture my mother's good luck charm. "You're out! We don't want you on our team. You can't talk or walk right. You stink!" he said. I picked myself up. My knees ached and burned from the fall on the macadam. With as much dignity as I could, I hobbled out of their midst. Realizing there was no private refuge in the schoolyard, I ran into the hall and down the steps to the basement toilet. I hid beside the piss and disinfectant smells of the latrine where I finally let my tears go. I vowed to learn their English better than they. Like Pinocchio, nothing would stop me. I could hear the song the children often chanted as they saw me shining shoes on the street corner near my father's shop. It sounded through the clouded glass and chicken wire window of the basement latrine which opened on the school yard.

> *Guinea, guinea goo,*
> *shine my shoe!*
> *I've got money*
> *but I won't pay you.*

I was going to school in America.

THE EXOTIC ENEMY

For all things original, spare and strange,
praise Him....

Gerard Manly Hopkins

We could invent love until the sea closed in. That's all
I was sure of in 1936 in Greenwich Village. Those were
dark years, but wild years for me. My father already
knew what Stalin and Hitler were up to, even if a lot of
others didn't. Us kids felt a vague threat hanging over
us. I dreamed of being a revolutionary poet, when I
wasn't dreaming of Molly—my pretty, plump and
graceful girlfriend. She had a skinny brother, called
"Nebby", who was nervous and decidedly unattractive
to females. No one remembered that "Nebby" didn't get
his nomer from nebbish, but from the first part of his
name, Nebekovski. Nebby was always worried about
the way he looked because girls paid no attention to
him. To become a big hero so the girls would like him,
he decided to run away and join the Spanish Loyalist
Army—but he was afraid of guns and didn't know a
thing about shooting one. Molly made me promise to
teach him how.

I was ashamed of any nebbishy guys of my
ethnos who were scared of guns, scared of the woods,
scared of worms when you took them fishing. Being
good at guns and fishing made me very suspect among
my friends in the city, but I fared well in the country
compared to most of the guys who were studying at
Stuyvesant High School. My father, a Turkish Jew, had
made a point of teaching me to hunt and fish. He
believed that every man ought to know how to defend
himself with a gun. He expected that any minute a

workers' revolution or Hitler's troops might arrive in New York City.

"Wars are fought to save rich people's money! People like us can get killed by their own govern-ments!" my father would bellow. After Stalin's purges were known and after Hitler started World War II, he would say the same thing—with more conviction and louder oratory. "So, why should only the govern-ment soldiers have guns? When the Secret Police come for your family, you got to be ready! When the whole world is one country, one race, one religion, one class, then you can be a pacifist!" He would hold forth as he taught me to aim and fire the rifles he bought me on my birthdays. He gave me two hunting rifles—just like his.

"You always need a spare—just in case—and you hide them in different places—one easy to find, the other impossible! You're not going to be a Socialist like the nebbishes in this city—always expecting a workers' revolution and scared even to kill a chicken! A gun's like a poisonous snake to them! They scream like girls if they only see one. They can't put a worm on a hook without throwing up! What kind of a man is that?"

I felt sorry for Nebby. I always thought of him when my father talked like that. I befriended him-- mostly because of his sister, but I called him Nebby, too. He was in no great position to protest anything anyone called him. I was proud, too, of being the tallest guy at Stuyvesant High School, the top public school for science and math in New York City --especially, it seemed to me, taller than the guys who were scared of worms, guns and girls--the ones the German guys who hung around the park drinking beer called "sissies." The Jewish guys, to get back at them, called them "Krauts," and "Beer bellies." Then they would retaliate

with "Kikes" and "Jewbagels!" Everyone was calling
the Italians "guineas," or "greaseballs," the Englishmen,
"fruits" or "limeys," and the blacks, "schwartzes" or
"niggers." Me? I was called the "Crazy Turk" because
I liked guns and hunting. But no one messed with me.

"I'm gonna' be a hero when I get back from this
war!" Nebby told me. "You'll see! Then all the girls in
The Party will like me and pay attention to me."

The main girl who was paying attention to me,
and I to her, was Nebby's voluptuous sister, Molly. I
was crazy about her. She had the exotic looks of her
pretty, blond Greek mother who was a nurse, and the
brains of her Jewish father—a busy doctor who tended
poor people's kids for nothing and taught courses in
medicine at New York University. Just like my father
did. Molly and I were from a liberal socialist group. We
weren't sexually repressed like most of the other kids at
school. Molly's mother had, on the insistence of her
father, supplied her with birth control devices. We used
to read Emma Goldman's and Margaret Sanger's essays
and discuss Free Love as a high and mighty ideal—like
Alexandra Kollantai of Russia! Molly and I became
totally obsessed with each other. I was in the throes of
the hottest love affair I'd known since discovering the
difference between men and women. We lived in
Washington Square. My father was a physician who had
written declamatory articles, for Emma Goldman's
magazine, *Mother Earth.* He supplied me with all the
knowledge needed, so I wasn't scared of making girls
pregnant or catching diseases like some of the other
kids at school. Ours was the only house in the square
owned by radicals and we had a tendency to shock the
neighborhood. I felt like a man of the world—taking
Nebby's sister into the attic of my parents' house as
often as I could. Molly and I were living a life of nubile

bliss—but Nebby felt very left out of all the fun in our crowd and Molly started distracting me from our love-making with worry about him.

"Please help Nebby learn to shoot a gun," she pleaded with me. "I'm afraid he can't defend himself. He swears he's really going to run away and join the Spanish Loyalists—and he's threatened to tell my parents all about us cutting school to come up here if I tell on him. I'm worried, because he's never even seen a gun in person for real!"

Molly was absolutely beautiful to me—with her blond curls and the roundest softest silkiest breasts and thighs and orgastic sighs in my universe.

So, I showed Nebby how to shot my gun. It wasn't easy to teach him. He tried hard, but he was just too nervous and scared of the thing. It made too big a bang and hurt his skinny shoulder when it kicked back. Whenever we finished practicing with my rifle, he claimed he had a terrible headache and had to rest. Still, I did my best to teach him—poor haunted, scrawny guy, dying for the girls to notice him, aching to be a big hero with a medal on his chest!

To my and everyone's surprise, he really disappeared one day, and Molly got a letter from him a few days later saying he'd joined the Spanish Loyalist Army and was about to become a real hero. One night, when Molly was supposed to meet me for a trip to the attic, she called instead. She was crying hysterically.

"I can't see you tonight or ever. I don't want to see *any* boys. We heard today that my brother's dead. I'm going to stay home every night after school to be with my parents, because they are crying all the time. They said I should have told them what Nebby was planning to do. I don't feel like making love anymore, because Nebby never will get to."

I guess I'm telling this story to make a little memorial to Nebby, I mean, Nevin Nebekovski, because now I'm sixty-six, and I still remember Molly. I remember wanting her for so many years, not being able to have her. I became a poet who writes about how deep the fascination with the exotic other goes—no sentiment about it—this passion with the blood of the other which stains our hands and tongues—this desire to poke at the fruit until its juices run, to tear the rose from its stem, scatter petals to the wind, to pluck the butterfly's wings for the microscope's lens, to plunge a fist into a teetering tower of bricks, watch the debris sail, explode fireworks until all crumbles to dust and is undone, open to the curious eye. Does this or that creature die as I die, cry as I cry, writhe as I would if my guts were ripped from the walls of my flesh, my ripe heart eaten alive?

Always the probing questions of sacred explor-ation—as if science can be progress without empathy. Does a penis feel as a clitoris feels? Do slanted eyes see as I see? Is a white or black skin or sin the same as a red one? Is it like me? Does it burn, does it peel, does it boil in oil or reel in pain? The obsession to possess the other so completely that her blood fills the mouth and you eat of her flesh from its bone, and then know if she, if he, feels as you feel, if your world is real.

Maybe, because Molly was exotic to me—we were different—she a Greek, me a Turkish Jew, or maybe because she was a blond with pale skin and blue eyes, and I, an olive skinned brunette with dark brown ones. Long after my hair turned grey, she remained an obsession that no woman—not my wife of thirty years— no woman—and I tried many before I got married—could erase. I still have dreams about her.

Molly's mother decided to go to church again

after Nebby, her only son, was killed, and her father, a Socialist, didn't approve. It broke his heart when Molly entered a convent and decided to become a nun. Thank goodness she changed her mind and left the convent for college! Her father, by then, had given up his medical practice here, and moved to Israel. A few years later, her mother left the West Side to look for him. I heard they got back together again over there, and Molly, when she finished college, joined them in Tel Aviv. That's where she taught school for forty years.

Yes, I'm sixty-six, and I can't forget Molly, and I know now that erotic ideas are like flashy lights turning on in heads that echo from mouths and shine up secret places, and people can be greedy in their groins and ugliness can come even from the beauty of nubile bliss. Sex can be ripped from the blood as if the body were not a house of green moss, a vase of kindness, a space for greed set alight from the dark by the glow of hand on hand.

And there are still the word wounds, like roots of mushroom clouds that could rise now from the pock marked earth: *guinea, dago, spick, nigger, polack, wasp, mick, chink, jap, frog, russkie, red bastard, kike, fag, bitch, macho pig, gimp, dike!* The stench of flesh could again follow the sprayed dust of children's eyes melted from wondering sockets, animal skin, thighs, men's hands, women's sighs roasted in a final feast of fire beasts caught like lemmings in a leap to Armageddon— false resurrection! Word wounds could rise from visions of charred lips, burnt books, paper ashes, crumbled libraries, stones under which plastic pens and computers are fried amidst the last cried words, smoke to pay lip service as all dust into dust returns....

I'm old enough to know, now, that the head is

fickle like history. An orchard, the body is free and soul invents itself in smile and song. I had a letter from Molly. I tried writing to her about a year ago—a love poem of our youth, and she finally answered me.

A letter came in the mail this morning from Tel Aviv. She's been a widow now for three years, like me. She said she's coming to New York to visit her grandson next month and she'll call me. We can have dinner and a talk, she says. She thought of me often through these many years. So many long years ago when we were young!

Nebby never got to be a hero—just a casualty of machismo—like me. Molly's worried, she says, about her grandchildren and the threat of nuclear end...."It would be worse than Hitler or Stalin, worse than anything Right or Left," she says.

Yes, we'll invent love until the sea dries up or tides flood over or the bombs explode human blossoms to dust, and poets are only madmen talking crazy and making sense.

BEYOND THE SPIT OF HATE

...Out of the mountain of despair
a storm of hope.

Martin Luther King

"Get outta ma room, ya black-as-Hell nigger!" Old Mr. Helms croaked loudly. I'll never forget his voice.

"Contrast creates perception." I remember musing over what my Haitian Healthcare professor had said in orientation class the day before. "Your Black skin will sure make that white nursing uniform look whiter!" She laughed. She was always teasing us. I hoped she'd understand that I was working my way through, and couldn't have my homework assignment done, my first evening on duty at the Borough Park Senior Care Center. I was on my way to quitting the ranks of the unemployed. Dressed in my new white uniform, I hurried down ten flights of stairs trying not to make a crease in my trousers. When I looked in the lobby mirror, I couldn't help smiling. I looked as handsome as the young Mohammed Ali. His poem: "Fight like a butterfly, sting like a bee," sang in my head. But I'd had to give up my amateur boxing nights at the gym to go to school. I was an official hospital worker. A clean cut figure in my new, ivory whites! My stomach felt like it was digesting red hot lava. No time for dinner. There was nothing in the frig. My guts were on fire with adrenalin surge.

I'd just earned my certification as a nursing-assistant at Brooklyn Community Tech. I was about to apply all I'd learned. By the time I'd showered and dressed, it was seven o'clock. I had thirty minutes to make it up Flatbush Avenue. I pulled my winter wool jacket on and hurried out the lobby into the freezing street. But it was exactly seven-thirty when I made my way through a cloud of disinfectant down the hall. I rushed to the sixth floor and got my assignment from the head nurse. I figured it would be easy, only five patients to worry about. But was I wrong!

Mr. Helms was a shrivelled old man, more wrinkled than the prunes Aunt May tried to make me eat for breakfast. His skin was a disgusting wax paper white with purplish veins showing through. His nearly nonexistent white hair stood on wispy ends. I approached him cheerfully: "Dinner tray time, Mr. Helms!" He opened his faded blue eyes and looked up at me with an intense quiver as if having a heart seizure.

"Get outta of ma room, you black-as-Hell nigger!" he croaked loudly. I stood astonished as he began to laugh. "I ain't never seen no nigger with square hair before!"

I must have turned as purple as his veins. I was struck with rage. I approached him again, silently, with the tray. A glob of saliva flew from his wrinkled lips catching me on the right cheek. I felt my face lose its shine as his spit met my skin. My burning stomach wanted to puke up my rage. My dignity seeped out of my pores. Wiped and enraged, I decided to move on and take care of my other four patients. Thank goodness, they were nicer than Mr. Helms, and two of them white as him, but how was I going to deal with him?

My impulse, after retreating to the washroom to wash his saliva from my face, was to let old shrivelled up Helms starve. Just sneak his tray onto his bed table as he dozed and let it remain untouched until collection time, exactly what I did that first evening. "Let him eat only *if* his day care is white!" I told myself. His laughter and voice had pierced my memory so that every time I looked at myself in the mirror, instead of a young Mohammed Ali, I saw a stupid square head staring back at me. One night I dreamed I smothered Helms to death with his putrid pillow, making it look like he'd died in his sleep. I woke up in a sweat deciding that letting him slowly starve was better retribution. What good was he to anyone anyway? Why should I fight him to help him live? But the lessons I'd learned from my Haitian professor about dealing diplomatically with cranky old patients kept running like a recording in my brain.

Finally, a different kind of determination possessed me. In that uniform, I imagined myself as a dove of peace. I remembered what my Black pastor had said on Sunday, after young Hawkins had been shot in Bensonhurst:

Don't let the beasts of the world turn you into one! Take up the white man's burden, he shoulders it poorly. The Black man's burden is so heavy no weak, white soul could carry it! Prove that you're more human than your oppressors. All life begins in the heart of our Africa. We are the oldest of people with the deepest of souls born of the longest suffering. We're born of of the black and fertile primary soil of our Africa and its soul music has become the teacher of the world! Alchemize hate to love.

Triumph in nonviolence. If we riot, they have an excuse to shoot us down in our streets, and our young die first. Dr. King taught that we must pursue non-violent change to survive. Praise our Black Immanuel! Praise our great Malcom X, too, who learned all people are equal before God! Be ready to defend yourself, by any means, if violently attacked. Praise all life born of our Africa! We shall overcome, we shall *overcome! We* will. *We will. We will....*

The next morning, with my rage turned to wits, I went out early and zipped over to Kmart on Fulton Street downtown. I bought me a white ski-mask. The kind that covers your face, except for your eyes. It was the dead cold of January and ski-masks were easy to find. In my mind I was rich as the deep black, creative soil of my Africa, source of all life. I put on my ivory whites.

In the corridor, outside old Mr. Helms's room, I donned my white ski-mask and matching white hospital gloves. I picked up his dinner tray and spread my elbows like the wings of a quick and dextrous dove about to fly into the path of a big old clumsy vulture. I walked into Mr. Helms' room, carrying myself like a dignified ghost and I *rapped* in a high jazzy pitch: "Mr. Helms, you got no one but me to help you tonight. Your guardian angel flew in to feed you right. This is your yummy dinner plate, cause love, I tell you, Man, is *stronger* than hate. Truth can be deep *black* and necessary, even if you think it's *all* white, white, whitey." I put down the old man's tray on his bed table and handed him the spoon. Wide-eyed and confused, he took it, looked up at me quizzically, and began to eat his porridge like Little Miss Muffet watching Spiderman. I repeated my routine every evening for weeks and he always ate his dinner. He even began smiling at my *rap* delivery. After a few weeks, he even rapped with me, banging his spoon on his table like a drummer and laughing a toothless grin. After a while I was able to quit the mask and gloves. He even asked me to give him a flat-top haircut like mine. I would've complied, but he didn't have enough hair for a good square.

Maybe something beyond Mr. Helms had made him a racist as a boy, but I fooled him with my wits, because he was pitiable, embittered, lonely, isolated, and dying, and I was strong and young and compassionate, on my way to becoming a professional. "You don't have to love all your patients. Don't even try, or you'll burn out fast. You just have to do the job and take good care of them," my Haitian teacher had said at Brooklyn Community Tech. Mr. Helms died quietly and peacefully in my arms one evening, nine months later when I was changing his soiled sheets and gently cleaning up his old bony body. I crossed his withered arms over his sunken chest and said a prayer for his soul to be saved from his waxpaper skin. Mr. Helms didn't make me rush to my supervisor to quit like a fool my first night on the job. He didn't keep me from my appointed rounds and he never will.

It took many years, sixteen, to get my medical degree and my own practice. Yes, I did it! I'm a statistic—a ghetto doctor born and bred in the ghetto. Mostly Blacks come to me where I chose to be, but sometimes, a poor white person has no place else to go, and Mr. Helms flashes into mind. When his spit haunts my Hippocratic Oath, I push him back into the deep recesses of my soul. I imagine him imprisoned in my heart chamber. I swim on like Shine, the legend of the Titanic. Helms's apparition is my guiding light. His hate was my triumph. I feel purified by the spit of his hate. It drove me to a powerful self-respect. The kind that covers your face with truth, and makes your pupils rich as the black soil of Africa from which we all began. I think of how all pupils are black and all corneas white and all eyes for seeing inward as well as out. When I think this way, tears come and I smudge them all over my face, making my black skin shine, washing away old Helms's spit, again and again.

LEARNING AMERICAN GRAMMAR

God is not interested in only the freedom
of black people or brown people or yellow people
or white people, but of all people.

Martin Luther King

I watch television every afternoon to improve bad English. I am been in U.S. three years. My composition professor says I have developing good vocabulary but sometimes conjugate wrong. I miss articles and my verbs are not agree. She gives me C+ to make me to work. She says I write with good details, but need better grammar. I study to be pharmacist. Good living. Americans buy many drugs. I live in Haitian neighborhood, downtown of Brooklyn, where I am believed as Haitian, though Pakistani.

I need better American grammar. I watch American television. Coming next a horror murder mystery: close-up of nice leg of white woman's pregnant corpse about to be cut by buzz-chain saw. A man stand at window in bloody butcher coat, vomit puke with chain-saw in hand. "Bear with me! "he say. "We're almost through!"

Another woman on T.V. looks like my mother at home in Pakistan, only lighter skin, looks into trash can behind brick building and screams horror mouth open, drops can's top with big bang. I hear her horror screams on and on. People all ages are dance suddenly and eat 'McMuffins.' Blood tastes in my mind as they leap and smile with burgers to happy lips sing: *It's a good time for the good taste of McDonald's.* I see only one dark-skin as me among them. I think of forests my Haitian friend says cut to feed cattle. I think of Chicago stockyards where many millions of steers every years get bashed in head with sledgehammer before throat are cut, bodies string up to drip red blood. I am become vegetarian long ago.

T.V. horror show is not real as rape of pregnant women by soldiers at home in Pakistan. Russian tanks. American bomber jets on the border of Afghanistan. Contra's called Freedom Fighters on T.V. news—cut pregnant bellies by bayonets in El Salvador. Channel 4 talk show host discusses *sodomy* in Georgia. Handsome homosexual, looking pale and nervous, tells how he has been arrest in his bedroom during act of sodomy with government official who go off free while he go to jail.

Old woman says: "This is a matter of human rights, not just gay rights, I don't want the police in my bedroom."

Talk show, gray hair host says: "Americans are not quite ready for brownshirts in their sex lives, even if skinheads are talking neo-Nazi slogans outside their windows." I don't know what he means, but I try to guess. What is a skinhead? I think a brownshirt might be a Nazi secret police. There's so much to remember in my studies at Long Island University. I achieve A's in science because I study every night very much.

I see many commercials very funny. Very far out, wow!

A newscaster interrupts for flash special. The Pope had welcome Waldheim to Vatican City. Protests rage all over Italy. Italians march with Jews against Pope. I remember Hitler had only one testicle. He rumor to be *coprophiliac*! He made anti-sodomy laws in Nazi Germany. I read this in paperback history book to practice my English when I first come to U.S. three years ago from Pakistan—but I don't go for sodomy. I don't like *hypocritic*, either. I like men and women together make babies, but I am afraid to invitation American women. The women of Pakistan cannot go out on "dates." You can only visit them at home with parents. If you do, you are proposal to marriage. I am not ready for wife. I want to "dates" like white Americans. But only with condoms. Americans talk of sex all the time on T.V.

A muscular white man in black leather jacket rides Honda motorbike with salivation smile. Punk-rock teeny-boop boogy with purple and green hair sticks out chicken-feathers Mohawk. Many earrings and bracelets like loud bells in close-up. She is dress in a small purple lace mini-skirt. I learnt these things, but I am not sure what skinheads are for. The Honda seal floods the screen with hardcore music big blare. The girl purple and green stick-ups hair says she lovers her bike, too, and ride off fast in cowboy boots down sparkle wet city dark street onto sunny country road in a second, distance fast.

Wife of house smiles at white sheets and white shirt her boy child made dirty with mud: *New Cheer does it every time!* News shows burned body of torture Chilean boy. Pinochet ship, Esmeralda, sails into New York Harbor, masts with white Christmas lit lights up and down for Liberty Day near nuclear gunboat, *USS Iowa*. President Reagan push laser beam button and lights renovation Statue of Liberty. Rockefeller Center Rockettes kick heels up to *Star Spangle Banner.* Screen bursts fireworks like the sound of seven tons of bombs that fall on Afghanistan. Make rain blood every day. South Korea students has been riot in the streets for democracy. New York City sounds like many bombs of blast. *AIDS Hotline* number comes on. *Do you know where your children are?* strong voice of man asks. Clouds of toilet paper argue who is softer, float like

Disneyland over blue and whirling world....

On subway yesterday evening, I trip into big strong white man in leather jacket with motorbike hat. I step accident hard on his black boot and he angers up to me and push me and says, "Watch your step, nigger boy," so only I can hear whisper. I change train. Forget about him to study. I stand near edge of platform, wait for C train to arrive impatient. Fifteen minutes past eight, someone pushes me hard from back as train yells into station. I pull up in time to save myself and see black leather jacket run away. Black boots. Motorbike hat off bald head. I move behind garbage pail on crowd platform where smell of urine sicks me as my stomach is up. Finally, the C train comes. I run on quick and doors slide close on my back. I grab first seat and remaining seats are fill by other tired feet. A color television picture of myself mugged flashes my head. I gaze out windows at lights coming on in the winter city. The sound of metal on the click tracks makes me almost asleep.

I am surprise to see only two other passengers, a white couple, left in the whole of train car. Mostly only dark skinned people are in this ride to my neighborhood. Sitting across to the door is a tall, thin teenager in light blue jeans. His long blond hair neat set as he gaze at the shining face of beautiful Hispanic girl of big gold earrings next to him. Very rounds and attractive. Big brown eyes gaze at him with love. Smooth light brown skin like my sister in Pakistan. Without any intention of minding his business, I look at them. The young lady was so beautiful with dark curled hair up high and big gold earrings. There is something interest about her eyes that I am not to understand. It made her amazing me. The blond lean gentleman with her has good shoulders like I wish to have if only I stop studies too much and sit. His dress was very nice, all light blue clean, but he is thin like me.

The train stop again to another stop. The doors open and see three black young mens to come in. They hold door and look in, then laugh and come in. They are dressed in heavy yellow and black jackets and baseball caps to backside and much gold jewelry. Two of them tall and one of them short and big around.

Immediate, I feel worry at them. I know something is to happen. They look at the Hispanic girl. They see she is beautiful. They begin to talk to each other. The three black boys look at the white boy. I could see fear rise up in the white boy's body. Suddenly one says, "Yo, baby, you got nice legs." He reach out his hand to touch the Hispanic girl. She quick pulled away and grab onto her boyfriend. The guys begin to laugh. "Whatcha 'fraid of black skin, baby?" he ask. I am afraid for myself. I cannot believe what happens. The worst part is I can't do something.

"Yo, what a fine girl like you doin' with a honky blue blond dude like that?" said another while walking closer to him. He slaps him on the face and pokes him on the head. The white guy is so scared. He begans to shake. He is not able to do something, because it was the three of them so big to him compared. He just sit quiet while the others picked on his girlfriend. They touch her all over her body. Up and down her silk legs. Up and down her sweater coat breasts and neck.

No one has the right to beat on anyone in a liberty country. That's why I come here. I see young Black Griffith boy killed by white Jon Lester in Howard Beach. Lester, born in South Africa, chase Griffith into highway cars, dead.

One black youth smiles and nod at me. "Yo, Bro. Want to cop a feel?" I almost yell, but look away.

"Dumb nigger," he says to me.

The three begin to grab the scared white boy all dressed in clean blue and bang his head against the train window behind him. Window cracks blood on his blue shoulders spat. They grab gold earrings from girl's ears. She scream with pain. They put hands in all the pockets of the white boy and take his wallet. I am next to be mugged. I am sure. I begin to stand up and a foot long dagger claps from one's pocket to the floor changing my mind to sit. The strength I need to be a man won't come fast. The train slows down.

"Drop dead, honky! You don't deserve this fine dark fox." One puts hand up girl's dress and she is faint nearly. The three black youths smile at me and nod and jump off the train. I feel worse. I want to help the guy but his attackers smile at me to approve. I stay in the car as they leave. I look at the girl. She turns to help her boyfriend who is bleeding down his head and face. She is crying. I try to go towards her for help, but she scream when I move to her, maybe because I am black skin, too. I stop and say. "Let me help!"

But she cries, "Leave us alone!" I don't know what to do. I look around and there is no one in the next car. The train stops again and she and her boyfriend run off. Blood drips on the floor from the love seat where they sat. The train is empty. I feel a war in my head, a war like a war in Afghanistan. Blood drips like hate at me. I am dark in my mind ashamed. "God is interest in the freedom of all people, not just white people or brown people or black or red people, but all people." Mohammed has said. I am good Moslem and believe this.

There is a revolution of the television potato chip not crispy enough and a man in a red drum suit plays a commercial rhythm. *No more whimpy chips! No more whimpy chips!* Everyone marches, singing. Then toilet Charmin papers argue who is softer in pink puffs over a blue and turning world. I wonder what is a skinhead for....

EQUAL OPPORTUNITY EMPLOYER

A woman of generous character will sacrifice her life a
thousand times over for her lover, but might break with him
forever over a question of pride....

Stendhal

"You really imagine you're the first man who implied that if I go to bed with him, I'll have the job, don't you? You really believe this is the land of the free and the home of the brave, too; don't you, Mr. Big Boss?"

He seemed to think he could kill two birds with one stone. I remembered my motto: "*Trust no one; least of all yourself.*" I'd been made the fool often enough. Painful lessons create cynics, so I lost my cool and completely blew the entire interview by refusing to accommodate what I was sure was his shallow lust for an exotic thrill. I stopped caring if I alienated him. I wasn't going to stoop to conquer this time, not again. I'd been burned too often by false flatterers.

"You think my having black skin and being a woman with a pretty face and good figure makes me dumb, don't you? You think I don't know what goes on in the white corporate world of C.E.O.? Well, no one's going to get away with trying to sweet talk this woman—before I even have my nigger *toe* in the door! Thanks for the invitation but no thanks! If you like my legs so much, how about letting me put them over the threshold of a corner office Monday morning, Honey Man, with a fat salary in my pocket, too, before you start telling me how you like my dress and can we go to dinner! What has that got to do with my degrees, my experience, my resume?" I stood to leave.

The sleek executive suddenly resumed his cool

demeanor. He hardly batted an eyelash when I lost my rational tone and dropped my proper English cadence to let it all hang out. "I can report you for a class action suit." I decided to jab it to him. "Are you still feeling sexy? Do you still want me to go to *dinner*?"

"Who'd believe you? Don't get all upset. It's not worth all the fuss and trouble." He answered very calmly. Or was he actually just exhausted—as he later told me.

"Please don't get all upset. Women have a hard time proving these things and it's not worth all the fuss and bother in this case, at any rate."

I became furious at his calm. "The fact is, I'm the best person for this job in this city, and you need your token Black and token woman. One stone; two birds! You're the one who blew this interview, as far as I'm concerned it's you who wasted both our time." I started for the door. I felt tears welling and I'd be damned before I'd give him the satisfaction of seeing me cry. I'd been building up to the interview for weeks—nervous as a cat about it. "You just lost your chance to satisfy the Feds with one bird!" I turned to give him one more disdainful look.

"I'm very sorry if I offended you, Ms. Angelvani. You're an attractive woman, it's true, and that would be an asset in this position. You are beautifully dressed and I simply meant to comment on how important that is for this sort of Public Relations position. What's so terrible about asking you to dinner to continue the interview? I'm starving, and exhausted. You've made it through all the bureaucracy and up to this third interview. Why get all hot and bothered over nothing. I certainly didn't mean to...."

I wanted to make him squirm a little, the way I had all week. "You're the one who's getting all hot and bothered; aren't you?" I smirked.

"Look, just because I gave you a compliment, said that you're an attractive woman, doesn't imply anything. You are an attractive woman and we need an attractive woman in this job—for obvious P.R. reasons. That's all...."

I didn't care to let him finish his sentence. I knew it was over. "Oh, can a Black woman do any good for the P.R. of this corporation? And what does our having dinner together have to do with anything? You think that just because I need a job I'll accept your insinuations...?"

He laughed, now, but helplessly. "You are a volatile woman. Calm down Ms. Angelvani! You really shouldn't go off feeling offended this way. It does neither of us any good, and I truly meant nothing but dinner and talk. I'm starving and it's been a long day." He went to the closet and took his coat. At least let me escort you to the elevators. My secretary's probably gone already.

"And you're a married man, too, according to my research." I softened just a little, because he was so disarming. I wondered if I'd been wrong.

"The fact is my wife and I are legally separated for over a year now. I just got the final word from her lawyer this afternoon that she wants to go ahead with the divorce. That's why I'm exhausted and off my guard. Her father is one of our chief shareholders, too. It's a strain all the way around. I've been eating dinner alone, late, every night for months. I simply thought it would be pleasant to continue our interview over dinner at the comfortable restaurant across the street where I always dine—so I could get a cup of coffee. Frankly, I'd more or less decided to hire you already, but I have two more girls coming in for interviews in the morning and it's too late to break the appointments. I have to be fair and see them, but..."

"*Girls!?*" I smirked disapprovingly. "You make it sound like you're auditioning a chorus line, or for a brothel maybe! *Girls*, indeed!"

Excuse me. You're right. I mean *women.* My slip. My daughter's in college and always correcting me on that one! My apologies. Again, no offense intended. Just a foolish expression. Maybe, I'm just feeling old enough to be your father. It has been a long day. I was impressed with your resume and the way you handled the interview, up until now, that is, but maybe it's my fault. Maybe I did sound insinuating. Your recommendations, your experience are excellent. It's a shame; this misunderstanding. We *are* really an equal opportunity employer. At least, we try to be."

"It wasn't the dinner invitation, so much as the tone of your compliments. I was sure there was an implicaton from your tone." I began to doubt my conclusion a little. Maybe I had been too hasty. "I'm usually right about these things. I don't know...." Maybe I've been nervous and overwrought about this interview. I didn't sleep much last night; it's true." Now I really did feel like crying. Maybe I'd blown it for no reason.

"My God. Did I imply....? Well, I didn't mean to, or maybe subconsciously I did and it revealed itself. It's been a hard day and a long lonely year, and I feel like a complete ass.... I, well, I.... I'm sorry. I....didn't know I'd implied anything. I don't think I meant to, but.... Well, you are attractive and you *were,* well, so *sympatica*.... Maybe I got carried away without knowing it.... What shall I say....I....?

He was attractive, tall, greying, distinguished, polite. I'd been tempted to accept his invitation right off. I was lonely, too, and I hadn't had a decent dinner out in weeks. I'd been job hunting like an obessessive maniac. Working at it every minute, every day. Employment agencies, telephone calls, head hunters, newsletters in the industry, research in the library, but this was *the* job I'd always wanted and I was worked up about it. I'd had such high hopes. I'd spent a day researching the company and its executives and preparing for the interview with him. I knew all his bio specs. Maybe, I was overwrought and over reacting to nothing. I decided that as long as he wasn't pawing me, I'd give him the benefit of the doubt. Even if it didn't work out, I'd at least have a good dinner for my trouble. I was fairly broke and hadn't eaten right all day. "Okay. My apologies if I misunderstood." I laughed to cover any tears that were welling. "Maybe I'm the one who feels like an ass..." I tried to laugh again.

"Let's just forget it. Even the best of us can make mistakes and misread things, or use the wrong tone. Dinner and some *talk?* About the position, that is."

"Okay." I softened my tone. "I'm starving too, to be very frank."

He became enthusiastic again. "Great. That's better. It's a treacherous world, out there; it's true." He opened the door for me, and stood aside so I could exit clearly.

"It sure is." I answered flatly.

I sipped that one wine spritzer very slowly. I wasn't going to let myself get tipsy handling him. But he really did order coffee and nothing to drink. We started talking like ordinary people. "My Black grandmother was Puerto Rican on one side and my father was Southern Italian. You're looking at four minorities rolled into one package." I laughed.

He laughed to please me. "A very nice package at that."

"You think so, do you? Well, I'm what the world could be if got its act together!" I laughed again and he laughed again to please me.

He convinced me to trust him, and, yes, I fell in love with him. Not right away, but a year later, after I'd been on the job for awhile. It wasn't just the romantic atmosphere of the restaurants we ate in, or his good looks, or position. I knew he really wanted *me*—not just a fling. You don't make love the way he did—*eventually*—on just a lark. His wife had been uptight and frigid and he'd been loyal to her for too long.

When we finally made love, after months of courtship, and conversation, it was like the sea rolling into a desert and washing shells of soft living inner bodies to shore, polishing their worn crusts in the sun. We felt like balmy night breezes after a sweltering loneliness of repressed heat. We were the Sunday sermon that makes trees grow greener and bees give honey. I felt healed in his hands as if he were molding me of clay. I made his pale face shine with sunny color. He called me his night orchid—blooming in the shade of his soul. I made him feel desire and passion like he'd never felt before. He was thirst and I was water—how can I say how wonderful it was without sounding purple! Who knows why. We made jokes about the *exotic* other, about making it with the *enemy* for a thrill. We'd both had plenty of history courses in the real world. We didn't kid ourselves. We knew all the psychological sociology of our situation. We were big city slickers with higher degrees. We knew what we were doing. We laughed about it all the time—and took it dead seriously, too.

But, his wife decided she wanted to keep him and her father owned a big piece of the company. That's right. You almost got it! But I didn't get fired. I just got transferred far away—to Atlanta—naturally. At my request.

People tell me I've got a bitter sense of humor and I do. Even my smile twists around a little before it shines out, now. It can't come out straight anymore. It curves around a knife that's lodged in my brain from a place that bleeds with red and blue light, slowly. It will bleed slowly until it kills me, or I die. But we all have to die some day anyway. I know he's got that same wound in his skull—left over from our passion— which will never come quite like that again—like a teenage love, unrequited in its requitedness—forever. Would I have gotten the job if I didn't have dinner with him? Would he have asked me to if I were white or ugly? Will I ever know the answer to those questions for sure? Did our colors have to do with our excitement?

I make an excellent salary for a woman, and especially for a Black woman, as a C.E.O. in Atlanta. I did get promoted—a good excuse for asking to be transferred. When I drive through the South, I pass through the poor Black shanty towns like the one where I grew up—Spanish moss hanging over the mud at the edge of every city or town—the shoeless children with no fathers. The old grandmothers rocking on the porches in squeaky old chairs, houses with no window glass, ragged curtains and shades flapping in the hot breeze. A rage bleeds in my brain from the knife lodged there, and I don't have much faith that anything but a hell reaching at heaven will ever exist here on this earth. Because I know not only the brutal, genocidal history of slavery, but the story of the bomb and Hiroshima, too.

And, the Rape of Nanking, the Spanish Inquisition, the Holocaust, Vietnam, Cambodia, Burma, the Philippines, El Salvador, the massacre of indigenous people everywhere, the rage of guns from South Africa to Nicaragua, Afghanistan to Angola, Yugoslavia to Los Angeles, the Hitlers and Stalins and President with their Gulf war massacres. History's my hobby. I read in the evenings, alone. I keep trying to figure out the *Guernicas* and the ovens carefully engineered for burning human flesh, even making lampshades, as if light can shine through murdered skin. Like the song says, Fire's what I knew with him. I have a bitter sense of humor. But people have to laugh.

I live alone and I don't love any man too much. I think about him sometimes, of course, as you'd expect—at night when I'm alone and not reading history books. He thinks about me, too, when he's alone at night. We know those moments—both of us, and we know that heaven can happen for a tiny moment here on earth—even if we're mostly living in hell.

Sure, he was blue-eyed and yes, it was interesting to love someone so very different. He said, so, too, and yes, I let him go, as clichéd as it sounds, *because of the children*—the daughters he loves. That's why he went, too, but also, because my mother and brother wouldn't have understood love with the *enemy* anymore than his snobbish old father with his weak heart would have. So, when I smile, it curves around a lot of history before it shines out. And always in the middle of his brain, in the middle of mine, when the night is dark and the damp orchids are sighing in caves of sleep, the wounds in our brains bleed purple and red, the same colors as our thoughts—as everybody's.

No, he really wasn't just a creep out for a cheap thrill. He is as lonely as I am and was. He's strong and decent in character. And no, he laid all of his cards out and left it up to me. Like a real gentleman should. It wasn't just a moment of weakness, and neither was he for me, because I'd been up and down and around the mountain already. We might have stayed together until we died—if it weren't for the rest of you—but the hassles would have been something—and there were the children and my mother and brother, and his father, with the weak heart getting older.

The money I send home is putting my brother through his Ph.D. in molecular biology—guess where—? At Harvard! He's going to make a little scientific history—on sickle cell anemia. He's on the verge of discovering some very esoteric thing about reality. And my mother's living real good on what I send her. I get a great salary and I work damn hard for it, too. The company gave me a medal and a big bonus at Christmas. I'm their equal opportunity asset, too! Nobody messes with me.

Him? He's still got his great executive position and his father-in-law and father are happy as a lark with his wonderful granddaughters, doing so well—though his father's old heart's getting feebler every minute. The kids are in high school now. He writes me whenever he's depressed, and I answer if I'm up to it. Sometimes we even phone—but only in very depressed moments. "I can't stand it," he says. "Please, reconsider?" We joke about running away to a desert island. But, we're too civilized to do it. His wife's in mid life crisis—naturally—and he's encouraging her to start a new career. To get out of the house. He's decent. So am I. What else can anyone expect of us, Tristan and Isolde? Romeo and Juliet? Othello and Desdemona? People have to live and love's not always enough. Sometimes it's got nothing to do with it—as that great

American philosopher, Tina Turner, says.

Anyway, contrast creates perception, like they say. You can only see light, if you know dark, and you can only feel pain if you've known joy. He and I; we understand all that and it was *my* decision, finally. My brother's Ph.D. at Harvard rests on a long slow struggle and I wasn't going to throw away that little bit of real history in the fire of love. That old Pandora must have been a woman like me! Ha! Because she held unto hope closing that lid just in time after she'd opened too widely her thighs. "*Trust no one; not even yourself,* " is still my motto, because the joker is wild and wounds us with our folly.

And like Doctor Du Bois said in 1903, "*the problem of the twentieth century is the problem of the color line.*"

ROSA IN TELEVISIONLAND

The soul has to stay where it is,
Even though restless, hearing raindrops at the pane,

The sighing of autumn leaves thrashed by wind,
Longing to be free outside, but it must stay....
John Ashbery

Rosa, a pear-shaped woman who faintly resembles an aging Sophia Loren, limps peacefully through Brooklyn's Red Hook section past the groceries or fruit stands of her usual route along Smith Street. She has no idea of the peculiar events that await her. Trucks are unloaded by denim clad workers as wooden crates filled with fruits and boxes of canned goods roll noisily down unloading ramps—aluminum wheels purring in the morning bustle. Groggy-faced children gambol toward a red brick public school which Rosa Della Rosa passes precisely at eight o'clock every weekday morning of her life. Rosa holds her head a little higher as she walks past the school, knowing that she was never able to attend it.

A school boy, just ahead of Rosa, stops to pick up a delinquent grapefruit which has rolled from a broken crate onto the sidewalk. He aims it at the seat of his schoolmate's pants. As the boys scurry into the schoolyard, Rosa bends down into the gutter to rescue the fruit and desposit it in her string shopping bag. "Only trees should throw food to the ground!" she exclaims softly, repeating an adage her mother learned long ago in Southern Italy, where the wasting of food was considered a sin against the earth. Rosa, by her act of salvage, hopes to redeem the schoolboy's soul from his naive prank, as well as have a nice piece of citrus for her breakfast.

As she stands, Rosa pats the bun at the back of her neck, which is held with a large Florentine hair-pin her mother brought long ago from The Old Country. She winds her long grey hair in the same way every morning and secures it exactly as her mother did her own. Not a strand is out of place. Her sturdy black Oxford heels serve her well as she boards the bus at the corner of Atlantic Avenue. She smooths her black dress and coat into place as she slides her seventy-eight year old body into the seat behind the driver— just as she has for over twenty-five years. Retirement has never once occurred to her. Her birth certificate was lost long ago in Italy. She simply pretends with the help of a worn baptismal certificate, that she's under retirement age. Since she works efficiently enough, the factory manager has never bothered to check into it. To the few faint hairs that grow on her chin, she pays no mind. Girlish vanities and dreams of romance have long ago faded with her fading irises.

"Rosa, you look beautiful and happy today! What's that spark in your eyes?" asks the bus driver who's seen Rosa board his bus every work day for the past ten years, from 1966, when he began working his morning route, to 1976.

"*Niente*. Nothing at all. I looka da same as yesterday. This dress is just like my other one. I wash one; wear one. Wash one; wear the other! Why do you joke? I found a good grapefruit for breakfast, so I smile more. But, it's a nice day, *si*?

"*Si*. Sunny as Italy!" The driver, an African-American, agrees.

"No, nowhere is sunny as Italia!" Rosa smiles and laughs, "except Africa. *Si*? But almosta!"

Rosa disembarks from the crowded bus full of screaming high school students and enters a small factory where she takes the elevator to the third floor, removes her coat and sits as she always does, every weekday morning of her life, at the end of a long conveyor belt which carries tiny boxes, row upon row, past her inspection. It's Rosa's job to make sure that each box contains exactly eight pieces of candy-coated laxative gum. Then, she takes lid after lid in her right hand, clamps it down with her left, and transfers the closed box to another conveyor beside her where it passes along to be automatically sealed in cellophane.

Rosa Della Rosa has worked in the chocolate laxative factory on Atlantic Avenue for thirty years since her husband died. She never thinks to stay home and collect social security, as it would be shameful to take government funds. Financial help can only be accepted from *la famiglia*, and the only family Rosa has left is her ailing older sister, Helena, for whom she cares. She was unable to have children with her husband, and now, all her family is dead, except for Helena, feeble and bedridden with whom she lives in an old Red Hook tenement apartment. Rosa's father declared long ago that any man who would have so little pride as to accept welfare is "a lazy bum." Rosa never managed to make the distinctions between hard earned social security, welfare or charity.

She lives in a world of simple infinitives where the answer to the mystery of life is: to wake to work to sleep to see to say to drink to eat to walk to go and to come, to be born and to die. She speaks only the minimum of English needed to get her through her evenly patterned days. As a girl, she remembers nearly starving to death when crops failed after World War I, creating a severe famine throughout Southern Italy. Her father, after the First World War, sick of watching his family's agony, worked and bartered his way to The

New World. A few months later, he sent steerage passage tickets from New York so that Rosa, her mother, and her older sister, Helena, could follow. Later, her brothers were brought, too, and finally, the whole family was reunited on Mulberry Street in New York. From that tearful reunion, they lived in a small, crowded apartment huddled around a coal stove in freezing winter and fanning themselves for relief on the firescape in sweltering summer.

The mid-morning factory whistle sounds, and Rosa gladly goes down to the basement for her coffee-break. She meets with her fellow women workers there, around an aluminum percolator, to rest and talk of husbands, children, family crises, and the price of food. Rosa, considered indomitably cheerful, always sits in a corner of the room nibbling her daily piece of anisette toast, now and then offering a bit of wisdom to the conversation. "Children, dey gotta have da rules, buta da rules musta be putta widda love from *la famiglia*." When the other women complain of their husbands' behavior, she always states, as if for the first time, "A man, he no can cry too mucha; is a woman's work to cry, to worry, to make a nice housa, cooka da food and lova da bambinos. Da man, he pusha here and he pusha dere, but he no can afford to cry!"

Since Rosa seldom says anything that can be debated, the younger women nod their head in affirmation, and continue with their chatter. This morning, the conversation goes differently than ever before. Domenica, a petite curly-haired brunette of forty-three, sits beside Rosa and speaks animatedly: "Listen, Rosa, I figured out how you can earn the money for Helena's hospital bed—the one I showed you in the catalog—so you don't have to hurt your back no more helping her to sit up! My nephew, Don, is casting director for a commercial television studio—ya know? Where they make commercials to sell things on T.V.? Well, he was over for dinner last night and he's looking for a nice elderly lady to do a false denture adhesive commercial, and I told him about you. He wants her to have a cheerful smile and a foreign accent and look like everybody's sweet old grandmother. 'I wish you'd give Rosa, where I work, the job,' I says to him! Because of your sister's hospital bed. He says, okay, he would use you if he could. I showed him your picture that I took with the other women—at Christmas—when my kids gave me that new polaroid camera. Don says you look just like his grandmother—my mother, Lisa, who passed away not long ago. I hadn't really thought about it until he said it, but it's true, you do. And Rosa, guess what? He's coming by this afternoon to meet you and maybe take you for a screen test. He says he'll make sure they pay you good, if he can use you!"

Domenica's dark eyes sparkle with cheerful enthusiasm. "Just think, Rosa, you'll be on *television!*" Domenica is proud to have something so exciting to tell every body, but Rosa feels embarrassed by the public admission of her need for money.

"Holy Mary, Domenica! Um no needa money. Uma save lidda by lidda. But, uma be so glad to meet you nephew!" Rosa feels that to introduce one to a member of one's family is to bestow a great honor of friendship.

When the work day ends, she rushes to the lavatory to wash her hands and recomb her hair into a fresh knot. As she carefully smooths down her black skirt and picks a few pieces of lint from it, Domenica enters excitedly. "He's here, Don's here! I saw him from the window!" She quickly hurries Rosa to the elevator and out onto busy Atlantic Avenue. A bright yellow taxi stands at the curb and a young, dark haired, fair skinned man alights from it. Domenica, short and olive-skinned, gives her tall blue-eyed nephew a warm hug and proudly introduces him to Rosa.

"*Mi piace! Piacere!*" Rosa beams.

"My pleasure, too, Mrs. Della Rosa." I think you might do fine for our spot, but I want to take you to the studio with me now for a quick test, to see how you come out on camera. I can take you right there in this cab and get you back home in a couple of hours."

Rosa instantly fills Don with nostalgic memories of his grandmother who died several weeks earlier. Don's grandmother was his staunch defender from the wrath of his parents all through his youth. When things were difficult during his teen years at home, he went to live with his grandmother who indulged him greatly with food, affection and approval. The smell of Rosa, a mixture of garlic and rose water, fills Don with a pleasant sensation of remembered solace. He immed-iately treats Rosa with gentle respect, despite her limited control of English. He decides to personally escort her through the entire job to make things easier for her.

"Me, get in a taxi?" Rosa shys away hardly capable of being persuaded to break the regular pattern of her day. "*Mama mia*! It's very nice, but uma go home to my sister and cooka da minestrone for her supper!"

"Oh, for heaven's sakes, Rosa, I'll stop by and look in on Helena and explain. I have the extra key you gave me to keep safe for you. I'll get her anything she needs until you get home. You'll be home soon, anyway.' You can use the money you make from the commercial for the bed to make Helena more comfortable. She'll understand. Don came all this way just to meet you!"

She lowers her eyes. She doesn't mean to insult Domenica or her nephew's efforts. She's seen just enough television to know what a commercial is, but she can't believe what's happening. The idea of a taxi ride fills her with trepidation. At last, she consents to embark with Don. The cab speeds quickly up the avenue toward the Brooklyn Bridge. As it buzzes over the metal groundwork of the big bridge, Rosa sits stiffly upright hanging on to the backrest in front of her. Accustomed to subways and buses, she's never driven over the Brooklyn Bridge in all her years in the city. Her dark pupils dart about as the huge cables of the bridge and its lofty granite arches loom over her. The sudden change in her routine puts her in a state of shock as Don escorts her into the television studio with its bright lights, chrome, cameras, wires, and bustling personnel. She can do nothing but stare, listen, smell, sense what's happening. Her heart throbs, but she smiles and murmurs. "*Piacere!*" assuring everyone that meeting them is her pleasure. She holds her worn black leather purse to her bosom to keep her hands from trembling. Still, they shake a little as they caress the familiar leather.

Rosa is placed before the camera at different angles and asked to smile and say her name. She complies humbly with Don's every wish.

"Well, Mrs. Della Rosa, the producer agrees. You'll do just fine. You'll be on camera for about half a minute and you'll only need to say one sentence. "

"...Which we'll teach you. Don't worry about a thing!" Don ads reassuringly. "We're taping on Monday at an old Victorian farmhouse in Morristown, New Jersey. I'll bring you there in a studio limousine."

Rosa's not at all sure about what the producer or Don are describing, but she understands she'll go in a car with Don next Monday to a place somewhere outside the city. What concerns her most is having to take a day off from work at the factory. Something she's done so rarely that the thought fills her with dread.

"Rosa, you'll make more on Monday than you make in a month at the factory!" Domenica is proud to exclaim aloud at Friday morning's coffee break. "Don says so!" Domenica stretches her small frame to its full four foot eleven inch height and smooths her curly brown hair as she stands beside the perking percolator.

"*Madre de Dio!*" Rosa crosses herself, though she rarely goes to church. She believes what her father told her: "Most priests are thieves who want to take from a hardworking man and his family, so they can have nice dinners with plenty of wine!" Her father, like his father before him, had wearied of paying indulgences to the local churchmen who ran his village in Southern Italy-- while The North and The Vatican seemed to grow richer on the back of the starving South. "Faith in God is infinite; but The Church is infinitely corrupt!" Her father often declared with passionate conviction, "Hail Mary!"

Monday morning dawns and Rosa, in wonder, sits nervously by her kitchen window, peering diligently out into the street for Don's arrival. She sips coffee and nibbles a piece of anisette toast. She has never ventured from the Red Hook ghetto of immigrant Italians with its rapidly arriving and integrating Hispanic community, since her husband died thirty years ago. She asks little from life. Ordinary daily bread is good enough and anisette toast to her is a great luxury. When she can't, out of agitation, finish the piece she's begun, she carefully wraps it in wax paper and puts it back in the bread box.

Around her, Rosa has watched soul after soul

writhe in the agonies of ambition. Though she's full of empathy for their miseries and longings, she's content to care for Helena and feed an occasional neglected child of the neighborhood or stray animal. She knows every family on her block, and all the local storekeepers. Sometimes she tries to comfort a widow with soup or herb teas, home remedies learned long ago from her mother. Rosa wrings an old lace and linen handkerchief and clutches her purse to her bosom as she peers nervously out the window through the fire escape to the street, watching for Don's car to appear.

The bun at the back of her neck has been more painstakingly arranged than usual. Rosa remembers the last time she left Brooklyn was to go to her parents' funeral in Manhattan's Little Italy. In their late eighties, they had died twenty years ago, within two days of each other, half frozen in the bad winter weather, when their apartment house furnace failed. Rosa is ashamed that she wasn't able to relieve their poverty beyond taking the burden of Helena from them. Her three brothers were better able to make money for the family, but they'd all been killed—one in World War II, another in the Korean War, and her eldest in a construction accident when he was sixty-three, a few years before their elderly parents died. As she sits vigilantly awaiting Don, she recalls that her food-bearing visits to her parents meant much in their old age, when they retired from factory work, but neglected to collect social security.

Rosa's husband was a mason, a brick layer like her brothers. One of her brothers introduced him to her, and when they were married, her husband brought her to live near his family in Brooklyn. Rosa's father was able to offer no dowry, as in The Old Country, so she felt fortunate to find a husband at all. Though Rosa earned money for the family table from her factory work, her father was always worried about her virginity and honor, and sorrowful over Helena's aging maidenhood, in a city whose customs he never really understood. He was greatly relieved when Rosa married, but Rosa's mother was heart-broken to have her daughter move away from their neighborhood village.

As the studio limousine speeds through the Lincoln Tunnel, Don remarks to Rosa how they are riding through a tube under the water. Frightened, Rosa holds her breath from the carbon monoxide fumes and fears she will drown under the Hudson River. To all Don offers, Rosa nods her head in constant awe, exclaiming, "*Madre de Dio!*"

With Don's help, Rosa finally alights from the studio car which brings them to a plush green lawn in the back of a huge white Victorian mansion in Morristown. Rosa sighs in wide-eyed wonder. Voluptuous sunlit shrubs, trees, flowers of every bright springtime color, sweet smells of pine and fresh mown grass surround her. This, she decides, at last must be the America my family was promised by the ticket salesman who came to our village—who sold us steerage passage aboard a steamship to The New World. This is the America bathed in golden light that lit our dreams as we rocked across the sea on our sickening voyage. This is the America my family never saw! Here the trees are as green as *Apulia's* olive groves! "Blue sky, sunlight like *patria mia*!" Rosa sighs.

"*Que bella! Madre mia!*" She gasps breathlessly to Don: "Um no can believa dis! Brooklyn es *brutto*, butta dis? *Simalare de Provincia d'Apulia! Bellisima*! Dis isa America uma dream when um holda my Mamma's skirt ona da cold oceana! Uma wisha

Helena coulda see disa! Uma wisha Mamma and Papa coulda see dis bella America! *Madre mia!*" Rosa crosses herself at the thought of her parents sharing the sight with her.

Don leads Rosa to the edge of a giant picnic table where she is greeted by a make-up artist who begins staring at her face, but not her eyes still wide with amazement. She's made to sit in a folding chair while she's powdered and rouged and lined with shadows."Ina my ola village, only a *putana* putsa paint ona *la faccia*! she jokes with the make-up artist who pays her no mind as he doesn't understand what she's saying. "Don't talk, it ruins the lips!" he commands. Rosa humbly stilled, thinks to herself how in Puglese villages along the Adriatic coast across from the Greek Islands, the women wear black dresses after their husbands die, and go to church every day to say the rosary. They keep their hair in a bun and work in the fields until they are too old to. Her mother never wore any powder or rouge, saying it was only for bad women.

As the make-up man continues to fuss over Rosa's face, she takes in more of the scene around them.

A long redwood picnic table is spread on the sprawling, manicured lawn around which tremendous pine trees loom in dark green splendor, accented against a clear blue sky. No factory stacks or noises rise in the distance. On the seemingly infinite table, Rosa stares in wonder at the plentiful food. Great roasted hams with glistening pineapple slices shining in silver trays and glowing with red glazed cherries. Platters of roasted turkeys, crisp and brown, stand beside bowls of cooked yellow corn dripping with butter. Great mounds of shiny fruit spill forth from gleaming porcelain bowls beside sparkling crystal goblets puffed with electric blue linen napkins. Sumptuous loaves of bread, rolls, pies, cakes, cookies of every description, bright ripe vegetables in abundant variety, are radiant with the cool sunshine of early spring. The air fresh and crisp, the tranquil countryside mesmerizes Rosa. "At lasta, uma see America ina my family's dreams," she remarks as the make-up man, who pays no attention to her words, finishes.

A cicada, singing in a nearby tree, makes the sound man curse aloud to break her spell. "If that godamned bug doesn't quit singing loud enough to be taken for a frigging buzz saw or a jet stream," he shouts to the director, "we'll have to end up doing a voice over back at the studio!"

Shocked out of her reveries by the coarse language, her visage prepared for the camera, Rosa is abruptly greeted by the director who immediately begins drumming a sentence into her head while the costume mistress wraps and ties a crisply starched, magniciently flowered blue and red apron over Rosa's plain black dress. The director makes her smile broadly and repeat the sentence over and over again, until she thinks her head will burst from the strain of stress and gesture. Don stands by and helps her drill until, finally, after several minutes, the crew breaks for a rest before the rolling of the cameras. When, at last, they pause, the powdered, smiling Rosa, in her brightly colored apron, can grin perfectly into the big red light on the camera, hold a lacquered cob of yellow corn beside her face, and say:

"Uma always use *Ultragrip* ona my dentures to enjoy my family pic-a-nicks!" During the break, while the prop girls scurry about putting finishing touches on the set, and the director gives commands to the several extras who will be used to represent Rosa's family, Don explains to her:

"There's a child psychiatrist and pediatrician on the set to supervise the children. They get paid $150 per hour!" Don points to a man and a woman beside several children and toddlers dressed in gingham country frocks and suits. There are two babies sitting in highchairs and several pseudo-relatives of every age now gathering around the huge picnic table. Don explains that they will pretend to be picnicking merrily behind her as she stands before the table to recite her line, smiling into the camera. "Considering the prop girls, director, sound and camera men, studio personnel, commercial script writers, our salaries at the ad agency, yours and the other actors' fees, remote control rig, trucks and transportation, this commercial will probably cost close to three-quarters of a million dollars to produce!"

"Holy Mother of God!" Rosa sighs in disbelief. "Um betcha da food alone costa alot a money! Did you ever see such a bigga table, such a bigga turkey ina you life?"

"Yeah, and not one 'spicy meatball' anywhere!" Don teases, smiling. "This is an All-American feast!" He enjoys Rosa's wide-eyed wonder at the incredible world of television into which he has benevolently brought her.

"Okay, Mrs. Della Rosa; ready on the set!" Calls the director.

"*Si signore*. Uma ready!" Rosa answers, practicing her smile at him. "Uma ready." She remarks to Don as he leads her to her spot on the set: "Uma lika to smile. You can take da smile from you face and put ina you heart, widda a feast lika dis in you eyes!"

All becomes hushed; then, at the director's cue, the pseudo-relatives behind Rosa, on camera, begin to gesture and laugh as if at a picnic. Rosa, as she was bid, holds up her lacquered cob of corn, smiles broadly into the red light on the camera and repeats her line: "Uma *always* use *Ultragrip* ona my dentures to *enjoy* my family pic-a-nicks!"

Cut! shouts the director, "Mrs. Della Rosa, the corn was hiding your face too much. Hold it away to the side of your face, with your pinky out more!"

Don explains from the sidelines in Italian. He murmurs reassuringly.

"*Si signore!*" Rosa nods obediently and moves the corn away from her face. She sticks out her pinky in a delicate gesture.

"Ready, cut two, take two!" the stage manager claps his board. "Roll um!" And so the process is repeated through several takes until the director is satisfied with the results.

"Okay, Cut and print!" He finally shouts and perfunctorily adds, "Thanks everybody. You can go home. Dismissed!"

Rosa can hardly take the smile from her face. It seems frozen there from repetition. The muscles of her cheeks ache.

"Well, Rosa," exclaims Don. "You're a star! You'll be watching yourself on television before you know it!"

"Helena will no believe when she sees me! Holy Mother of God!" While Don tends to business, Rosa sits exhausted on a bench at the edge of the picnic table. She watches the prop girls begin to dismantle the set. Too excited to eat breakfast or lunch, her ordeal now over, Rosa's mouth waters at the glorious repast. Before she can even think of tasting a morsel, the prop and set workers begin shoveling the platters of food into huge, black plastic garbage bags. Rosa's eyes gape in silent horror as breads, rolls, pies, cakes, corn, vegetables, fruits, and amazingly glazed hams are swept from sight, bagged as garbage. In utter disbelief, Rosa sees the feast of her dreams unceremoniously destroyed, shoveled into garbage bags, thrown to the ground.

Finally, unable to contain herself, she asks quietly: "Whadda you gonna do widda dat bigga turkey? Uma know a nice orphanage ina Brooklyn...."

The prop mistress is used to being asked such scavenging questions by perpetually starving actors dismissed from sets. Without giving Rosa even a sidelong glance, she answers contemptuously, "Throw it away with the rest of the perishable props, of course! Salvaging perishables from sets complicates tax matters. Excuse me." She reaches over Rosa, grabs the turkey platter and slides the sumptuous roasted bird into a black plastic sack full of cracked and crumbling pies, cookies, and squashed fruit. It lands with a sloppy thud, spraying soggy crumbs over Rosa's flowered apron.

Don reappears as a costume girl bids Rosa to stand while she removes the apron. As Don escorts her home through the Lincoln Tunnel again, she doesn't exclaim anything in Holy-Mother-of-God phrases. In her mind, she sees the food of her dreams behind the house of her dreams shoveled into a huge black plastic mouth of hell as her starving parents and Helena and her brothers and herself, as a child, look on with saddened faces, somber with shadows of death.

"Well, Rosa, what do you think of Television Land?" Don questions cheerfully.

"*Non capisco nulla di niente. Non capisco, Signore. Non capisco.*" Rosa utters softly. Don decides she is weary from her exciting day, as she rests back against the cushions of the limousine, her eyes half-closed. When they arrive in front of her tenement home in Red Hook, Don helps Rosa out of the car and to the door, thinking that she is tired just as his grandmother would be after such a long and eventful day. "Will you be all right, Mrs. Della Rosa?"

"*Si, molto grazia, Signore. Gracia mille.*" Rosa puts her hand on Don's arm as if in sympathy and nods weakly. She enters her hallway without turning back. "*Buono notte!*"

"Good night to you, too." Don watches her grey hair disappear into the darkness.

She slowly climbs the stairs to her apartment and, in the dim light of the landing, opens the door, depositing her keys in her worn black purse which she leaves, as always, on the old hall table. She peers into the dusky bedroom where Helena wheezes quietly in her sleep. Without turning on any lights to brighten the twilight kitchen, she goes to the sink and washes her hands with soap and cold water—because the hot water tap hasn't worked for years like the one in the bathroom does, but it's too close to the bedroom and sound of hissing pipes might wake Helena out of her pain filled respite from slow dying.

Rosa goes to the bread box and extracts from its near empty depths the waxpaper wrapped, half-eaten piece of anisette toast leftover from her breakfast at the window. She sits again at the sill and peers into the coming night as slowly she chews the dry bread with her quite good, very old, real teeth, crushing it crumb by crumb, morsel by precious morsel.

HOT DOG ON THE IRT

Wealth is attended by power...
and hence oppression.... May we
look upon our treasures, the furniture
of our houses and our garments and
try whether the seeds of war
have nourishment in these our possessions.

John Woolman, English Quaker

Abigail Stewart wrapped in her shabby black mink coat curled into the corner of the rattling IRT Express as it rumbled downtown toward the Long Island Railroad Station in Brooklyn. Her latest and greatest grief welled in her throat with the touch of emphysema that choked her. Her pearl necklace was hardly visible beneath the folds of her coat and withering neck which she always kept covered to hide her advancing age.

"Time annihilates everything. There's nothing left for me now," she sighed. It had taken all her strength to drag the large alligator suitcase in front of her knees onto the downtown express. The doorman had helped her get it into the yellow taxi that brought her to the train station. She had deliberately avoided the crowds at Grand Central to go downtown to Brooklyn's Long Island Railroad Station where she hoped to enlist a porter to help her carry the suitcase onto the train. She had just enough money left from her allotted monthly trust fund allowance to take a train out to Southhampton, but not enough for the limousine she preferred.

As usual her charge accounts were as overdrawn as her lips. Her pale ears and waxen visage were assaulted by the clatter of the wheels and singing of the breaks as the train veered around a bend in the cold damp tunnel to screech to a halt at Nevins Street. Not even the three shots of bourbon Abigail had downed for breakfast succeeded in steeling her frazzled nerves for the perilous journey. Indeed, the alcohol had only succeeded in loosening the strings of her heart to hum a plaintive tune drowned in despair and the noise of the subway.

Three shivering men ducked a leak in the subway platform's grubby ceiling to enter. They sat, exhausted in the middle of the nearly empty subway car, not seeming to notice Abigail Stewart hunched in the corner behind her alligator bag, hidden in the folds of her black fur. As the doors slid shut a draft of freezing dampness penetrated the torn seam of the fur beneath Abigail's right armpit. Her mink had seen better days and so had her eyes now dull. The chill sent a shiver up her thin bones. Her waxen face sank deeper into the despair which pinched the corners of her eyes and knitted her furrowed brow. Still, one could see the finely wrought features of a face that had been a classic of British beauty of its heyday.

Tyrone and Clifton Washington were brothers who lived together in the Gold Street projects of downtown Brooklyn, not far from Bedford Stuyvesant. Guido Stalloni, who accompanied them, lived in the Redhook slum nearby. Guido had met Tyrone in Vietnam and later, again, in the V.A. hospital in Brooklyn where they went for therapy for their drug addiction and respective injuries—Tyrone's dizzy spells and Guido's broken knee cap. They were on their way to Coney Island to pick up a stash—the only way they thought to make money for their supper. Clifton, a perpetual college student, was Tyrone's younger brother. He'd lost his job a week earlier for sassing his white boss too proudly and so condescended to "hang out" with his depressed brother, Tyrone, and Tyrone's Vietnam buddy, Guido.

Tyrone, Clifton, and Guido felt their stomach ache with hunger as Abigail felt her heart shatter in the loss of her only friend whose burial was the purpose of her trip. His elegant interment was a picture in her confused psyche. She didn't even look up to notice the three men enter the car. Her mind was set for a long lonely journey dedicated to grieving her lost love. Images of his panting breath steaming in the cold air filled her mind's eye as he ran toward her down Park Avenue on the wintry morning preceding his collapse. He leapt into her arms to kiss her cheeks with wet exuberance. His lively joy in running freely towards her down Park Avenue was the only excitement to ornament her life for many years. All the adventure and trial of her existence had brought her to this lonely moment on the IRT headed to Southampton for his funeral and burial.

"He'll have the best my credit can buy. If only he'd not died just as my monthly allotment ran out, I'd be taking him to his rest in style." Abigail mused at the added irony that her dearest friend had passed at that difficult end of the month time when her allotted trust fund check usually ran out. So, Abigail had done something she tended to do towards the end of every month: ride the New York subway. By the ironclad stipulation of her mother's will, Abigail received only a carefully budgeted monthly allowance from her trust which her mother intended would last Abigail for the rest of her life. Abigail's great-great grandfather had accumulated the Stewart fortune in slave trade, a guilty family history that had driven Abigail's mother to be more charitable toward the United Negro College fund at her death than towards her only daughter, the last remaining Stewart in their family line.

"You see what I see?" Guido asked Tyrone.

"What you flappin' yo mouf 'bout now. Can't you see um tryin' to git me some zzz's?" answered Tyrone. "You done kep' me up this whole trip wif yo house music blaster. Lemme sleep, Bro, Stomach's as empty as this car and rumblin louda than yo' irritatin' voice. My belly skin is stickin to my backbone and this seat is colder than a witch's tit."

"Man, you're dumber than a junkie. While you're snorin', my brain's brewed up a way to git us some eats so we don't have to wait 'til we pick up and unload a hot stash for them loosey punks that steal our profits. Don't you see what I see curled up down there in the corner, hidin' itself in a mink with a big fancy suitcase parked at its patent leather shoes? Look, an old witch waitin for a rip off of her stash. Easier to pawn than a bunch of Columbian gold or smack, crack or icepop. I see an easier breakfast than takin' the heat in Coney Island. You understan' what um tellin' you, or is your brain froze to the window sill? Lift up your grizzly head and look down there to your left. Ain't that a nice lookin' suitcase what a rich lady in a mink coat can spare? She's got enough wrapped up in that coat alone to buy her six million breakfasts. She don't need that alligator bag, too. She'll never miss it. More of a misdeamor than a felony compared of what you cooked up. Direct your doped eyes on the cash!"

Tyrone felt his belly skin suck closer to his backbone as Guido explained his scheme. He replied with less enthusiasm than Guido would have him muster at 5:30 A.M. The January thermometer had dipped to a wind chill factor of 10 degrees below. "Stop flappin' up a dumb scheme, man. I seen that old lady the moment we got on. Leave it alone, Bro'. There's enough wind blowin' in this rattlin' tomb wiv out your lip blowin' up some more stupid shit. You know we got a job to do that's goin to net more than breakfast, if we git it done like we been told by the man."

"Come on, Tyrone! I'm interjecting here with Guido's projection. Maybe he has something under our noses not requiring such risk as a trip to that Coney Island den where we should be ashamed to make money from CIA crackers who ship drugs to ghetto dealers to commit genocide on black men. Let's grab the case and run. A mink coat can spare an alligator skin. Maybe there are some nice items of clothing or jewels in such a fine suitcase. She looks like a classy old lady too drunk to scream or even care if her bag disappears out the door at the next stop. There's a labyrinth at the Atlantic Avenue stop. If she moves to disembark for the Hampton trains of The Long Island Railroad, as I expect she will, we politely offer to carry her heavy load for her. The least we gentlemen can do? Don't you have any lightbulbs popping on in your grizzly head? Be smart and let's get busy. The train is pulling into the station, designating our destiny quicker than you can decide anyway, Tyrone. I'm with Guido, so move your bones, Man. We're on. You do the grabbin' and I'll do the gabbin'. She's starting to stir herself up. I can smell the pickled breath from afar. Move, Guido, quick, before you trip on Tyrone's soul. I'll ask a polite question and confuse her while you run up the stairs, left and out the junction exit. We've no time to think. It won't hurt a mink to lose an alligator. Go!"

Abigail raised her dampened, half shut lids to look up into the face of a magnificently smiling man who spoke with perfect British diction, as if he were a butler about to offer tea. Clifton Washington, dressed in a neat suit and tie and London Fog raincoat, was always ready for any occasion that presented itself. He had spent a semester here or there at a city institution of higher learning, perfecting his impeccable Standard American accent, as he had aspirations to escaping the Hell zone of project life to the other side of the IRT tracks, headed up the Eastside someday toward Park Avenue. He intended to disembark before reaching Harlem, a ghetto created by eighteenth century servants of the upper Manhattan rich. "Excuse me, Mam, may we please help you carry your bag to the train. We imagine you might enjoy being relieved of such a burden, as we surmise you are no doubt catching the train to the Hamptons as we are. You look so tired, we'd enjoy being helpful. We're Jehovah Witnesses from The Watchtower. Can I offer you some of our literature?

Clifton always kept some little religious magazines handy in his large coat pockets for such convenient schemes and he imagined he offered comfort with them, to the souls of the rich whom he was fond of relieving of their burdens. He fancied himself a modern Robin Hood in his own debonair way. He was well read in English legends, as his schooling had assured it. "We'll carry it for free and for three mere dollars donation, you can have these meaningful magazines that will set you on a path to the true God. You'll help us earn ourselves a cup of coffee to share. We are so very thirsty and hungry this freezing morning. I'm sure a lady like you will kindly understand our hungry plight. We really need some bread and would be happy to oblige you. A mere three dollars, please, would earn us all a very much appreciated breakfast, if you'd be so kind as to accept our porterage."

Abigail in her muddle thought she understood, but wasn't sure, and so she was about to ask while reaching for her money in the small purse she wore across her shoulder under her coat, when one of the three seemingly gallant men standing over her quickly relieved her of the tremendously heavy burden she was about to drag out of the opening doors of the car as the train entered its station. Guido and Tyrone departed ahead of her nimbly porting her alligator bag between them, as Clifton bowed gallantly before her and extended his hand. Before she could manage a garbled word from the delusion of her alcohol insomniac night of grief, Clifton offered a final nimbly uttered word.

"Thank you kindly for the wherewithal, Mam. We are so glad to be able to relieve a nice lady like you of her burden. We'll port it right on for you, on and on..." Clifton quickly exited after blocking Abigail Stewart's path just long enough for the doors to slide shut in her bewildered face and the train to resume its rumble through the dark tunnel toward Avenue Z.

"You's a clever man, Brother Clifton," Tyrone admitted as he met him a swiftly achieved platform away. Let's make it to the IND and out to Coney Island quick, before the cops start lookin' for our asses."

"You have put me in the mood for some fast aerobic walkin', Bro'," Guido smiled. I'm dreamin' bout bacon and eggs over lightly with hot rolls dripping marmalade and butter."

"Um dreamin' bout some nice jelly-roll for dessert, too, soon as we reach the pawn shop on Mermaid Avenue." Tyrone perked up.

An hour later, Daryl, Tyrone and Clifton stood over a fiery oil drum under the Coney Island boardwalk of a deserted beach near Neptune Avenue. The fire they'd started with beach refuse crackled with needed warmth. "Who'd think I'd end up havin' to eat an old dead dog for breakfast instead of what my dreams were congerin' up. What you suppose that old rich witch was doin' with this ole dead white sheep in her suitcase?" Guido groaned.

Tyrone moaned. "I knew yo flappin' breeze was gonna make us some trouble this mornin'." He put his back closer to the warm fire.

Clifton agreed, " I should known better than to listen to your gorilla brain so early in the morning before I've had my tea!" He wrapped his London Fog closer around him and rubbed his leather gloves together over the fire which flared up as it bit some beach oil amidst the newspapers and garbage within. "Are you really going to cook this pedigreed English sheep dog, you fool?"

"You damn right I am. It might not be bread, but it's still food, if you use your imagination, Bro. What you think we ate fightin' in Nam? I ate some damn roasted dog more than once over in Saigon. It ain't half bad!" Guido, to save face, was determined to make use of his backfired scheme.

"That silly woman was probably on her way to that animal cemetery I saw once in Southampton last summer before I got chased by the cops for skinny dipping on the town beach at 4 A.M. I'm not sure if it was my nakedness or naturally dark tan that bothered them more and thanks to my nibble feet, I'll never know."

"Roast dog's an oriental delicacy in Nam, even suited for a gentleman in a suit and tie with a vast vocabulary like you, Clifton. Um, hungry and um eaten. Waste not, want not the Bible says. It's a Christian lesson."

"One damn roast dog's better than three damned hungry dogs. Um havin' me some of dis hot IRT dog fo ma breakfas' cause the evidence will be gone and we still can pawn the suitcase when the case cool down. I didn't lug this load all this way for nothin' Meantime, Guido's fire keep us warm, Brother Clinton."

"Well, there you're correct. It's genuine alligator, and you are about to devour a dead English sheep dog which hasn't been dead for long according to my nose. Cook it well, Guido, to avoid salmonella. Too bad you don't have some of your garlic and oregano with you. If you don't do it well-done you'll be running your tail to the pot every minute for days and the entire fortune you've gained could possibly be lost on Kaopectate, green and ugly tasting stuff, which might end up being your just desserts."

"Now quit leanin' on me, Clifton. Nothin' ventured nothin' gained is always my motto. We might'a done better, it's true, but you still get a third of the alligator hock and we can still head out for the stash after I eat me some Hot IRT dog and dig me a hole for the rest.

"It was not the funeral I wanted for him. Not at all!" Abigail wept to the policeman who escorted her in her grief uptown to Park Avenue. "Where oh where is my dear Barker? He made me feel so safe."

"Just give me an accurate description of the men and the bag, Mam, and we'll do what we can, but we have a lot more important things to attend to in this city every second than the loss of a dog carcass, you'll have to understand!"

"I'm trying to understand, officer. Really I am, but I lost Barker so suddenly late last evening and haven't slept a wink since. Abigail's tears were sopped up by her tattered lace handkerchief as the officer escorted her, near collapse, to the regions of her own precinct to file a report. "I called the cemetery in South Hampton and they were all prepared to receive Barker early this morning for his burial service. He was the only family I had left. I don't know what took him so suddenly."

Geraldo Rodriquiz, Abigail's building superintendent, was at that moment discovering that a rat had stolen the poisoned cheese he's left in his basement trap. He lived in the cellar apartment of the old building on Park Avenue where Abigail Stewart had lived for sixty years. His new baby's crib had nearly been invaded by a rat which had taken up habitat in the basement of his building. He and his wife had the cellar apartment free with his job, but recently, the old building next door had been renovated to make way for newly gentrified modern cooperative apartments, and a population of rats in the building which had lain abandoned and warehoused for a decade, had taken up residence in the Rodriguez home. The rat which stole the cheese was attacked by Barker behind a garbage can, where it nestled eating the large hunk of tainted cheese. Barker, barking as usual, had run into the alley away from his mistress, just long enough to bite the rat's mouth swollen with cheese and come gallumphing back to her. He leapt up to greet her and wash her face with cheesy kisses, just before they headed up Park Avenue and into the lobby, past the doorman's tipped hat, as Abigail entered as usual, just after her dear beloved Barker's morning run. Even as Barker died, rats had crept close to the Rodriguez child's bed setting Mrs. Rodriguez screaming for her husband who checked his empty trap and added another hunk of poisoned cheese to a dark corner of the basement apartment on Park.

As Geraldo reset this last trap, a policeman drew his revolver on Guido and Tyrone. Clifton, headed for the Mermaid Avenue pawn shop, had just taken off down the boardwalk with the empty alligator bag. His good dress and speech had charged him with the task of getting the most cash for the goods.

"How many times have we told you guys not to start your fires under the boardwalk. Move it out!" the policeman shouted as Tyrone ran quickly away under the walk. Guido, with his broken knee cap was left to face the music.

"I'm so grateful to have Barker back for his trip to dog heaven," Abigail told Howard Kunitz, the proprietor of Animal Restland, as he recited a specially composed elegy over the soul of the deceased Barker. Abigail imagined Barker floating up on a cloud with his panting breath vaporized amidst crepuscular beams of light and the organ swelled above Howard Kunitz's modulated voice. "Dearly Beloved," he intoned as he ended his elegiac recitation over Barker's coffin, bedecked with white carnations and purple orchids, Abigail's favorite floral combination.

THE POOR SUCKER
AND THE BAT OUT OF HELL

Lunatics, lover and poets
are of imagination all compact....

Shakespeare

When we are adolescents, I now understand, the body turns anxiously to the flesh—rushing and rolling sprays of wind. Hopes ooze between our damp fingers, concoct heat, search for the zone and we come anxiously together with the breath sweetly askew. My boyhood friend, Walter, spent a good deal of his adolescence literally trying to suck himself off. When I look at the cat chewing his tail, I think of Walter.

"Three little words: I love you!" I'd sing a popular love song, changing the lyrics to tease Walter. "Three little words. Go suck yourself!"

"Yourself is not a little word, Jerk-off!" Walter would snarl back indignantly. Walter confided to me how he'd tried unsuccessfully to twist himself into a pretzel the way a Yogi might. He was never quite able to reach his goal with his lips as he told it, but he tried many times, bending and working to get his body round and around. He read reams of Yogic philosophies. One day, he even showed up in school holding his head to one side with a very stiff neck.

Pretty Boy, the class Romeo, was different. He could get all the girls giggling like a pack of hens, pecking around him, teasing him as he teased them, but Walter was shy with girls.

"That jerk-off beats his meat every night, I betcha! Walter complained of Pretty Boy. Walter was very good looking and built like a weight lifter. Many girls did their best to loosen him up, but nothing worked. Whenever the girls tried to talk with Walter, he'd run and hide his head in some wild, romantic love poetry.

It was during the time of the notorious Bruno Richard Hauptmann trial. Hauptmann was accused of kidnapping the Lindbergh baby, and he was about to be fried for it. The kids in our class at Stuyvesant High pinned a sign on Walter's back, because he babbled so much. "Hauptmann is innocent; Walter *is* the Lindbergh Baby," it said. Walter got angry and went home from school in the middle of the day and probably tried to suck himself off.

One summer, Walter got to know Tennessee Williams for real—at Lake George where his parents used to rent a cabin. Walter kept asking me to come for a visit at the lake, but I'd met Tennessee Williams at a bar in The Village and decided I wasn't interested. One week Walter finally convinced me to come for a visit to Lake George. He said Tennessee wouldn't be there because it was his parents' week to have the cabin. So, finally, I consented to go with Walter to the lake. He was so anxious all the time that I felt sorry for him—and, actually, he was very bright and an interesting babbler. We got to the cabin under the trees in a pine grove by the lake and the door was bolted locked. Walter tried to unlock it with his key, but couldn't. We were supposed to go fishing, swimming, boating, and hunting in the woods for snakes and bugs—all that stuff I loved to do—but Walter pounded and banged on the door and refused to give up. Walter's German shepherd, which was always at his side, started barking it's toothy head off.

Suddenly, the door swung open and Tennessee Williams walked out with about five other guys—each more queer than the others as far as I was concerned. Tennessee apologized for over-staying his time share of the rental. He was soft spoken and gentlemanly. Walter never seemed to know if someone was making a pass at him or not--woman or man. Most would have realized that Tennessee was gay, but not Walter. As soon as Tennessee walked off under the trees with his friends in tow, I turned to Walter. "See, I told you so!" I iterated the words with the usual obnoxious satisfaction such a statement brings its soothsayer. Walter had insisted that Tennessee was straight as an arrow, probably because he was too busy rolling up into a pretzel to notice anyone else for real.

But, Walter knew everyone in The Village—even more than I did—because he would wander the Lower Westside at night, his dog always at his side for protection. He was so close to that dog and always claiming he wanted to be with girls—but always walking that damn dog around The Village at night and sleeping with it—hugging it in bed. We used to tease him that he was making it with the dog, and he'd get furious. Walter was from a well-to-do family and he could always be counted on to buy somebody drinks or dinner or put them up for the night in his parents big penthouse. Also, he had these eyes, big and wide, that invited everyone to fill them with their ideas and dreams. Big eyes just sat in his head asking question of everything he saw and everyone he met. Those staring innocent eyes never seemed to comprehend anything, but Walter babbled on philosophically about every-thing—because he'd met and listened to every kind of artist that ever came to New York City to stalk the streets of Greenwich Village at night. He'd heard everyone of them expound their theories and philos-ophies, and he was very articulate at spewing them forth—mixing them up and regurgitating them with great charm—like baby babble and pablum--all at once.

I think what fascinated me about Walter was his utter innocence. It seemed that no realization would ever penetrate his mind or psyche with stark reality. He was all dreams, ideas, hopes, imaginings. He'd rather practice his peculiar brand of Yoga than face the real live viscera of a woman. I couldn't help him understand that getting into a woman was the best thing of all. I always considered masturbation or anything like it perverted, at best, beneath my dignity. I was extremely intimate with my cute cousin who happened to live with us. In the laundry room, in the pantry, in the closets of our house in Washington Square—whenever her father, my uncle, wasn't around. She was young and utterly nubile and crazy about me. I could bring her to ecstacy in an instant it seemed—just from kissing her breasts or putting my fingers in her juicy place. She was like the apples and grapes of Eden to me—all women and Eve rolled into one package of absolute pleasure. I was thinking almost constantly of sex in those days—but Walter, though he was a Hungarian with a brain as sharp as the best of them, remained hopelessly innocent when it came to real meat and potatoes. I avoided Walter when he talked about his pretzel antics and nirvana, but somehow he depended on me to keep him in touch with reality. He knew somehow that I was seeing the world as more real, even if he couldn't.

The autumn of our eighteenth year, Walter experienced a horrible tragedy. He was closer to his mother than anyone in his family. She was a beautiful and youthful woman of forty, but looked more like twenty-five, and oh, did she love Walter—her favorite son. He was everything to her. One reason I used to like to visit Walter was that she would serve us dinner—dressed in a pink silk negligee that Walter's father had brought her from one of his trips to Paris. He was an international businessman who owned a string of hotels to which he was always traveling with his two older sons—leaving Walter and his mother alone at home. His older brothers were tough hard guys—completely the opposite of Walter who was his mother's baby. Where Walter's father was always complimenting Walter's older brothers for being wonderful men, Walter's mother was always having to defend Walter from his father's sarcasm.

I remember Walter's mother had gorgeous breasts, and she would wear that pink silk negligee almost falling open all the time. I loved to get a gander at her cleavage as she bent over the table serving us a delicious roast.

Well, one afternoon, Walter's mother died suddenly just after a hysterectomy—a stroke after surgery. That evening, he begged me to spend the night at his place—with his father and brothers. He said he felt like he was about to flip out completely and needed someone besides them around. He begged me to come and spend the night on the couch in his penthouse on the Lower Eastside where his father and brothers were grieving.

"I can't believe she's dead! They said she got an embolism. What's an embolism? I expect her to be there at home." He'd told me he felt like the ground was disappearing from under his feet and he would fly off the end of the world. I really wanted to go home to my own house, my room and my cousin who lived with us--but I felt sorry for him. His eyes seemed more questioning than ever—and I had no answers to offer and no comforts from any gods.

That night, as I lay on the couch in that big

drafty penthouse on the Lower Eastside with the windows open and the white curtains blowing in the moonlight, I heard a huge scream come from Walter's room and it took a moment to recognize his voice.

"There's a bat in here flying around. Help me!" He screamed. I ran into his room and sure enough, there it was. A bat was flying all around Walter's bedroom, trying to find its way out of the window, but the curtains kept blowing in its way. Finally, Walter and I grabbed a bedsheet! His eyes were bigger than ever, bigger it seemed than the moon, full and shining in at us. We threw a sheet over that damn bat and Walter was holding it down like it was a raging bull or something—bending over it in his nakedness. He'd been startled out of bed by the bat's wings flapping in the windy room. You could see he was crying over his mother and feeling like he was going to flip out.

There I was helping him catch that bat under that sheet and there he was screaming and his big pet dog, the German shepherd, the one we used to tease him that he was making it with instead of girls—that dog came running into Walter's room and slipped and the dog's nose went right up Walter's ass as he was bending there holding down that bat out of hell under that sheet. Walter fell over and the bat flew free and Walter just screamed and kept on screaming and wouldn't stop screaming. Finally, the bat flew out the window and Walter tried to follow it. I held him back. His brothers came running in and had to hold him down from flying out the window after that bat. His father finally had to call Bellevue, because his brothers had to tie him down to keep him from killing them. We had to wait for the men in the white coats to come while Walter snarled and wept. Finally, they took Walter away to Bellevue. I never saw him really right again. He spent the rest of his life half in and half out of asylums, wandering around The Village with his dog, or sleeping in Wilhelm Reich orgone boxes. One day I heard Walter had flown out of the window, claiming he was a bat going to meet his mother in heaven or hell, calling her name as he flew down twenty stories crying to the moon. And I don't think he ever really got to suck himself or anybody else off—man or woman.

Years later, I understood that death in its brutal cruelty, coming and coming, shouldn't be a fear, but a final orgasm—the end of a curving line beginning forever in a circle. I wrote a mantra for Walter—inspired by Allen Ginsberg who we used to hear reading in coffeehouses around The Village when we were young. I recite my Kaddish for Walter, remembering our days of adolescence: *Touch the palms of your hands to a warm body. There's a tingling of sympathy in the hand spread firm on the naked flesh erect with the joy of the nipples. There is a tingling of sympathy in the tongue pressed in the ears and mouth, hollow with loneliness. There is a magnanimity in the legs spread and the arms opened. There is a tingling empathy in the body held by the body held and pressed, holy holy holy. Rama, rama, rama. Our mouths are holy, our licking and sucking and feeling and kissing and loving and touching are holy, holy, holy. Rama, rama, rama.*

A YAWN IN THE LIFE OF VENUS

Women are the books, the arts,
the academies, that show, contain and
nourish all the world.

Shakespeare

Venus stood on the fire escape of her brownstone apartment on Mac Dougal Street, brushing her damp auburn hair in the dusty New York sunlight. Venus was thinking how she should see a podiatrist about her perpetually aching metatarsals, but probably never would. She knew that they were *metatarsal* arches because she'd just read an article about them in a magazine she'd bought at the supermarket. It explained that 85% of people over thirty, living in civilized countries, where shoes and concrete plague human feet, suffer foot disorders, while only 7% of those in lands like barefoot India or China have foot problems.

"That culprit, the high *heel*! Invented most likely by the French!" mused Venus. "It's not only a device for mincing femininity and over-civilized grace, but a horror to the human spine thrown out of line by it and an utter anathema to the metatarsal arches!" Venus, an expressionist dancer, sighed as she thought of how people walk upright and not on all fours like the animals they are. She shrugged about how she ought to see a podiatrist but never would, and she smirked—realizing that despite knowing the caloric value of every conceivable American comestible from the learned backlog of ten years of unsuccessful dieting—she'd probably always be as hopelessly plump as a Botticelli Renaissance vision.

Venus Picatelli, perched on the fire escape of

her Greenwich Village apartment, was gathering glimmers of sunlight on her face and a glimpse of some backyard greenery as she lived on one of those Old World blocks where city gardens still exist as an institution, though they might be travesties of English or French gardens of past centuries. She'd just washed her hair with a green gel shampoo, and rinsed and dressed it with a bit of the contents of an aluminum tube of yellow lanolin manufactured by the oil glands of some dead sheep somewhere.

She was combing damp tangles from her long hair with a translucent, purple plastic hairbrush as she leaned over the backyard greenery growing on the patch of dirt in the garden below. The sun still managed its age old dance patterns on the laden branches of a lone Ailanthus tree planted eons ago. Its large, fern-like leaves were once again tinted with the light green of early spring as it lifted its limbs upward to where Venus' somewhat callused toes—with their shiny pink nails—stood out against the black wrought iron of the fire escape. As Venus stood on her black lattice shell, her pink toenails and purple hairbrush gleamed quite a bit more brightly than the pale cheeks and lips which she lifted to the reborn sun.

Her hair was exactly the same color as Botticelli's *Venus* as she yawned and stretched, letting it hang down the fire escape like Rapunzel's, but, alas, no one attempted to climb the sunlit locks of the thirty-seven-year-old Venus of MacDougal Street. No handsome young prince stood in the garden below, where he might have gazed through the metal slats of the fire escape up her short terry cloth robe to the naked crotch of her soft, slightly parted inner thighs.

Venus heaved another sigh and drew her head up so that her damp locks fell to either side of her too pretty face which was coated with a sheer flesh colored make-up, from a pink plastic case, decorated with imitation goldleaf, Florentine filigree designs. As her mouth yawned wide, the sun glinted from the gold platinum underside of her capped eye-tooth and pinched tiny wrinkles into the corners of her squinting sea-green eyes.

Venus was totally unaware, at the moment, of the life she was leading inside the head of Walter Goldbrick as he sat playing Schubert lieder and singing: "Green Is the Color of My Love," into the dusty keyboard and yellowed sheet music on the piano of his New York apartment a few blocks away on Houston Street. Walter thought of Venus with her reddish gold hair, plump and naked before him, on the sagging couch of his never-converted, convertible sofa, sewing buttons on his one light-weight spring jacket which would now have to be dragged from the back of his dusty, walk-in closet where he had stored it last winter. Of course, the picture of Venus lying languidly on his sagging sofa—pink-nippled and sewing on buttons—flashed quickly by amidst the notes of the plaintive song and gave way to the image of Venus sprawled, legs open, on the blue permanent-press sheets of her bed. Walter Goldbrick dreamed of Venus as he sang until he groaned a wonderful moan—just at the end of the Schubert song and slumped over the piano, breathing rather heavily. He felt the music rack caress his forehead with a thud.

The bump brought him back to the practical world wherein he knew that on Friday night, when Venus' daughter was visiting her estranged husband, he would, indeed, make his way to her bed via some theatre tickets and a late-night supper. "Ah, Venus," he thought, "without you, this poor *alte cocker* would be a very depressed old man!"

Walter Goldbrick, after all, was a ripe fifty-three years, making him a good sixteen years Venus' senior. He sometimes found it difficult to imagine the fact that when he was sixteen, and having nocturnal emissions, Venus was only a mewling, puking infant. So, he tried not to think about it. Instead, he thought of how proud he was, as a somewhat homely older man with graying hair and a long nose, to have such a young plump woman for a steady, if occasional, companion in love and romance.

He'd met Venus Picatelli at a film festival where young artists' films were being shown—a cultural event produced by himself. He was something of an entrepreneur of the arts who had never made it big or accumulated wealth. Still, he worked diligently for the young hopeful talents he helped to foster. He was a man of great taste living in relative squalor—the sort of fellow whose sympathies went out to others though he never seemed to receive his rightful due of affection in return.

Yet, as he sat there, in his ever-so-slightly ripped tee-shirt, playing Schubert lieder, he felt like a man who'd lived and was living through the body of Venus. The thought made his cheeks glow just at the moment when Venus feeling lonely and dull, her pale face yawning, stood on her wrought iron shell. She never dreamed that, at the very moment, she was leading a rather exciting life in the mind of Mervin Holst, a writer of nonfiction articles concerning the vanishing wilderness, acid rain and ozone contamination.

Mervin lived in a tiny apartment on the teeming lower East Side of Manhattan. He sat at his dusty desk, rifling through his files, looking for an idea which would sell at the springtime of the year and thinking of Venus. She flashed into his mind when he came across a note on how brown bears would not copulate when the cars passing through State Parks made them nervous and belched too much carbon monoxide into their lairs.

Mervin Holst always called Venus to check on the cocktail party schedule of the social circle of which they were both a part. They had met at a literary party for a book on the wilderness which Mervin had edited for a big publishing house. Mervin liked Venus' wit which she declared she seldom displayed when not in Mervin's witty company. Her wit was all Mervin allowed himself to like about her. She was too strong-minded and plump for his taste. He had a definite preference for young, tall, and very slender women, more in the shape of Giacometti sculptures than Botticelli paintings. He liked women to be very much younger than his forty-seven years, silly, and ultra-feminine, so that he could overpower them in bed. He was definitely a *leg man*, not a breast, buttock or belly lover. Venus' legs were too plump for Mervin's taste, and the one thing he could never forgive in a woman was thick ankles. He liked thin ankles with an almost Victorian fervor, the kind of obsession which caused skirts to be draped over music parlor piano legs to eliminate prurient thoughts at *musicales*.

A tall, barrel-chested fellow who towered above Venus' mere average height, Mervin wanted women to look frail as young boys, because he had a very strong mother, and making love to a strong-minded and bodied woman would be too much like making love to his mother whom he visited every Friday night in order to get his hair washed. Mervin's mother was, he had decided, the only one who could get all the soap out without getting any in his eyes, and his eyes, he had decided, were very allergic to every sort of available shampoo.

When he came across the note in his files about bears not wanting to copulate near traffic, he thought, for some inexplicable reason, of Venus in bed with Walter Goldbrick whom he had perceived as muscular for a man his age. He admired the muscular arms, neck and intellect of Walter. It was quite pleasant to think, just for a passing moment, of Walter copulating with Venus. He knew carbon monoxide wouldn't stop them. He imagined them in a bed of twigs and leaves, grunting and groaning like bears and growling in ecstasy. He liked them both and it was a brief vicarious pleasure to think of them all sweaty, smiling and grunting like bears.

Mervin Holst went on with his search for an idea which would sell at the spring time of the year to one of the ecology magazines he wrote for. He pulled out his bear file just as Venus was half way through her fire escape yawn, never realizing for an instant that she was leading an important life in the mind of Dolores O'Hara. Dolores was a forever-aspiring, forty-year-old painter who lived in a loft on Prince Street in Soho. She was busy mixing sea-green acrylic paint for the wildly abstract painting she was thrusting herself into that afternoon.

She thought of Venus' eyes and how they had glowed the first night she made love to her in the loft bed of her painting studio—the aroma of linseed oil and acrylic all around them, mixing with the feminine perfumes of their bodies. It was the first time Venus had allowed herself to live out her not very compelling fantasy of making love with another woman. The time had been right for it! The political climate set the stage! Women's Liberation allowed Venus to have the courage for the experiment. "There are many obscenities in the world, but any adult human being making tender love with another adult human being—so long as there's no unhealthy buggery—is far from the worst. I feel murdering dolphins or polluting with plutonium is far more obscene and the government does it all the time! But, it's never good to fool Mother Nature! And none of us would be here at all if it weren't for heterosexual love. I don't approve of straight bashing!" Venus had expounded.

Dolores lifted her sea-green paintbrush and slashed it across the middle of the canvas, thinking of Venus lying in bed, her sea-green eyes smiling a piercing smile and whispering: "I don't think I could ever be a lesbian, because I can't imagine not wanting to be close with men; but I do enjoy talking with you. Your friendship means a lot to me. Women ought to be able to be good friends, not just pitted against each other for male approval. We should have a buddy system, too, for professional networking like, 'the old boy circuit.' I think of Sappho and the ancient Greek way. She affectionately trained women to serve the Goddess. They developed camaraderie and then matured into wifehood and relationships with men. I think I have an infantile fetish for a mothering breast despite all liberated views.

"Don't we all?" Dolores countered wryly. "We all start out as suckers, and a lot of us end up that way."

Venus laughed. She liked Dolores humor. "I mean, don't you think there's a *puer* or *puella eternus* in gayhood, perhaps? I mean in the natural order of things. Most lesbians I meet had terrible fathers, but I loved mine."

"Mine was a wife beater. I hated him. Men!" Dolores made a sour face.

"Then, again, it might all be hormonal, so who can be punitive and judgmental about such mysteries?" Venus sighed.

"Most people!" Dolores answered flatly, in her characteristic tone. "Especially legislators." She'd met Venus at a women's rally for abortion reform at the State Capitol in Albany. Dolores had done the posters for the event and Venus was performing a benefit dance that night, a la Isadora, on the mall in front of the governor's offices, in order to attract a crowd for a demonstration.

Venus, like the first of the nine muses, Terpsichore, was a dancer who made a living from occasional performances, but mostly from teaching dance exercise classes in her apartment every morning. She'd developed a system of dance preparation known as "The Piccatelli Technique." It was designed to release the natural voluptuousness of the dance and was fairly well respected among avant-guarde dancers in the city. Venus had just enough students to keep her basic financial needs in order.

Dolores, when she'd met Venus at the mall in Albany, felt it was love at first sight. They drove back to New York City together in Dolores' station wagon full of feminist posters. Venus ended up spending the night in Dolores' Soho loft. Dolores made gentle, feminine, attentive love to Venus. "Women understand each other's bodies better than men can!" she told Venus as she showed her a poster she'd hung on the wall, titled "The Discovery of the Clitoris." Dolores had ordered it from an advertisement in the back of a magazine named, *Never Just Mrs.Again!*

Dolores O'Hara, who was an aging, abstract expressionist painter, a gentle if sardonic person, was easily satisfied with the smallest pleasures. She splashed sea-green paint onto her canvas and thought of caressing Venus—soft bosom to soft bosom—in the same moment that Venus, on her not-so pearly shell was in the exact middle of her lonely yawn in Greenwich Village, never dreaming for a mere instant that she was leading an adventurous life in the psyche of Pat Sampler.

Pat Sampler, a hosiery salesman, was on his way to Poughkeepsie to show his new pantyhose samples to a department store buyer there. As his eyes concentrated on the white line unfolding before him along the expressway, he day-dreamed leisurely of Venus with whom he talked often on the telephone—more often than in person—whenever he was in New York. He thought of himself, dressed in a pair of pantyhose, while being caressed by Venus. He imagined her forcibly holding his thighs open and raping him in the most exciting scene he could fashion. The white line drifted into his subconscious as Venus invaded his consciousness.

He lay on the bed of his mind in his long auburn wig and beige pantyhose and groaned with pleasure. Over his pantyhose, was the most exquisite pair of lace bikini panties he could imagine from Bloomingdales and stretched across his flat hairy chest was a padded, pink satin Maidenform bra. Pat Sampler was a transvestite, though quite privately, who liked to have strong women make love to him while he costumed himself in women's attire, but he did not desire sexual union with men. He couldn't help day-dreaming of what had never actually taken place between himself and Venus, though he longed for it to. He'd met Venus because he'd read an article about her views on the dance in a local feminist newspaper and sought her out to tell her he shared her opinions. He liked her, and her looks, and offered to supply her with Danskin leotards at wholesale prices, for the rest of her career.

Aside from enjoying buying Danskins wholesale for retail to her students, Venus liked talking with Pat Sampler. His voice was very feminine on the telephone, and she'd forget that she was talking to a man and talk to him as if he were one of her girl friends. They would laugh together about feminine foibles and talk feminist politics and art. Pat Sampler was a very well-read man, especially for a hosiery salesman. He felt starved for talk with someone who possessed a higher grade of intellect than most of the people he dealt with daily. Venus understood him. He'd confessed his transvestism to her and she'd made him feel accepting about himself.

When he'd explained his fantasies to her, she'd listened attentively and asked empathetic questions. She made lighthearted jokes about how he could turn into a woman like Jan Morris or Christine Jorgenson, and she'd become a man like Virginia Woolf's Orlando. Then, they would marry and live happily ever after. He enjoyed dreaming of the idea, though he knew it would never happen. On his lonely long driving trip—watching infinite white lines—dreaming of Venus made him feel good, just at the moment when Venus was partly through the mid-mark of her yawn never thinking for an instant that she was living a romantic life in the mind of Mike Mizre, her college friend of seventeen years.

Mike had decided that Venus was his only *true* inspiration and the only *real* love of his life. He'd had a long and arduous affair with Venus in college, back in the days when he was directing college variety shows and editing the campus literary magazine and Venus was a budding dancer who dabbled in composing romantic love poems, too close to nineteenth century sensibilities to be appreciated in the 1950's—in America.

Michael had enjoyed playing Svengali to Venus' Trilby for three years, advising and inspiring her dancing and writing, and producing theatricals, which inevitably starred her as the dancing gazelle of the campus. He decided, after several years of trying, to forget the passionate affair which was the mutual undoing of their virginities. There would never be another love like theirs in his life, he'd decided. They remained friends after the hot tears wept over the death of their love ceased to pour forth from the bottomless well of Venus' eyes. Michael had been the best man at Venus' wedding. He'd found he preferred being loved by men than loving women. "It," he reasoned "was so much simpler and less complicated than having to pick up the tab all the time, or having to remember to say, "I love you," or worrying about fathering children, while in the act of bodily relief supplied by love-making.

His fantasy of Venus included their sitting before the fire in a woodsy New England retreat—he, typing his latest hit Broadway musical and she, reading the pages hot off the typewriter, mentally choreo- graphing the dance numbers which would capture the essence of the leading *femme fatale*. "This is absolutely brilliant! You are unquestionably a genius! A hit if I ever saw one!" he imagined Venus' gesticulating with grace and dramatic vigor. Then he imagined retiring to his room where his handsome young house-boy would minister to his sexual needs before he retired for the night wherein he would sleep the sleep of angels in the arms of Venus. She'd cuddle close to him like pure and innocent child through the night. He saw her as *Innocents Abroad* in a Henry James novel.

It was that very fantasy which nestled in his day dream as he came across a picture of Venus and her daughter at the beach last summer. The snapshot was caressed between the leaves of the book he had been reading: *The Short Stories of W. Somerset Maugham.* Just as he found it and drifted into revery before the New England fireplace of his mind, glowing in the eyes of Venus across from him, Venus was quite a bit through her lonely yawn on the fire escape of MacDougal Street. At that very same instant, Venus was living quite another life in the mind of Luciana Kelly, her five year-old-daughter.

Luciana, having just fallen off her tricycle, was nursing a bruised knee on the sofa of her father's apartment on the other side of Greenwich Village. Luciana, who always missed her divorced mother on the weekends she spent with her father was imagining her mother hugging and comforting her, putting stingless, strawberry medicine on her bruised knee. She was thinking how it just wasn't the same to have Daddy fix a scraped knee as it was to have Mommy do it. Venus always made Teddy Bear talk like Donald Duck, but most of all, she hugged better. "I want my Mommy!" she began to howl making her father feel quite helpless. As he reached for the antiseptic spray on the bathroom shelf, the vision of Venus cooking spaghetti on a Sunday afternoon with Luciana playing in her highchair at the kitchen table flashed before him. The smell of pasta burning on his own stove may well have been the cause for his aching memory, or was it the stinging sensation of guilt he felt whenever Luciana cried for her mother, combining with the words "No Sting" on the label of the spray he took from the shelf?

"I want my Mommy!" howled Luciana again, just as Venus nearly completed her yawn above the

Ailanthus tree, never for one vague instant knowing that Finley Roosevelt Jackson sat at the desk of his furnished room, casting her in the role of a sympathetic "older woman" undoing his hopeless virginity.

"Don't be afraid, Finley, " Venus was saying in soft, sensuous tones, as Finley sank down and placed his tired, bespectacled head in her healing lap. "I'll show you how, and everything will be all right. Don't worry if you can't do it right away, I'll teach you how to make love, my darling. I live to give pleasure."

Finley Roosevelt Jackson was a young Black man recently come to New York City from Alabama. He was an extremely bright, well-educated, boyish man of twenty-six whose courageous mother had worked for years as a hospital aide to put him through college. His mother, who was not a political activist, but a hard-working widow, had trudged to work everyday to be able to send her only son the money he needed for his studies at Berkeley. Seeing his diploma had been her motivating dream. One Sunday morning in church, just before Finley was due to arrive home from California, Mrs. Roosevelt Jackson sat listening to a sermon on Civil Rights, the "Freedom Riders" of Selma, and the restaurant "Sit-ins" of Birmingham, when a homemade bomb planted by a local member of the Ku Klux Klan went off and demolished the church, killing five of its occupants, she among them. Finley, who had just come out of the heady atmosphere of final exams, and been graduated with honors from Berkeley, arrived home with his diploma in hand to find it was too late to show it to Mama. Broken hearted, he'd left Selma soon after and migrated to New York.

One lonely afternoon, because of his interest in culture, he was taking a walking tour sponsored by The Museum of the City of New York. On that tour, he met

Venus who was friendly and enjoyed the comments he made about local history. She'd been impressed with the way he seemed to know more about urban history than the tour guide. They'd lunched together after the tour. Finley, with Venus prompting him on, confessed his life story, loneliness and depression in New York. The black radicals he met considered him an Uncle Tom because he wasn't an activist with an Afro and Harlem diction. He didn't get along with his prejudiced white boss, where he worked as the token black in the office interviewing clients at a State Employment Agency, either. He was between the devil and the deep blue sea and rather unhappy about it when he met Venus.

She was empathetic and oblivious to her own voluptuousness as she voraciously devoured her lunch across from him. They'd exchanged telephone numbers in Platonic fashion and promised to keep in touch whenever an interesting walking-tour came up. Venus had no sexual designs on the thin young man whom she found intellectually stimulating. She'd no idea, as she completed her yawn, that she was undoing his virginity, nakedly caressing him in every possible way, upon the bed in the furnished room of his mind.

On a lazy, lonely, sunny afternoon in early spring, she couldn't know, that like many respectable feline, slightly bovine, beauties, she was leading several lives, all in the space of one yawn. She stretched and reluctantly bent low to climb into her window. She felt, not exactly bored, but in some way unfulfilled, unexcited by the possibilities greeting her in the eyes of all she knew. Even if Venus had experienced seventy different orgasmic thrills in the minds of sixty different people during the course of one yawn, she was lonely the way the human spirit is always alone, afloat in its boat of skin upon the sea of eyes that greet it, masks and mirrors reflecting the wondering and wandering image of love, the wry smile of a goddess who refuses to answer with more than a whisper of wind through the fresh greenery of spring leaves on Ailanthus trees, or the glint of sunlight off the silvery underside of a capped bicuspid.

Venus stomach growled. She thought of the leftover *Moo Goo Gai Pan* from last night's Chinese take-out dinner. She went to the refrigerator, opened it, and peered in at a cardboard container which sat dribbling gravy down its sides. Wistfully, she dragged the container from its shelf and plopped its gelled contents into a frying pan. She added plenty of soy sauce to revive its flavor. Then she sat with her aching metatarsals and legs out-stretched on the kitchen table and ate, wielding a big soup spoon, as she balanced the pan with its warmed-over contents atop her ample bosom, just under her chin. When she finished, she stood and expelled a burp and a bit of flatulence.

A little smear of gravy still on her chin, she took a soiled sack of laundry from the closet, yawned again, in the midst of several fantasies, and descended the stairs of her brownstone apartment building to the basement laundry room, squirming the whole time with the thought of the roaches which always scurried away in droves as she entered, and flicked on the bald light bulb hanging from the low ceiling.

As she listened to the slish-slosh of the washing machine, Venus thought about all of the people whom she knew—about how they were all decent people, gentle in their way—unique people who would never destroy or deliberately hurt anyone. She thought of how much knowledge, intelligence and understanding they possessed among them, how each one of them, from transvestite to lesbian, from homosexual to heterosexual to virgin, were, in their way, moral people with delicate spirits and open minds. She realized, too, as she opened *The Village Vocalizer* with its headline about some strife in Korea and Viet Nam, that none of them, including herself, might ever personally do anything about stopping wars, hunger, or injustice short of making contributions to The War Resisters League, or marching in demonstrations.

Standing there, in her *Cross-Your-Heart, Maidenform* bra, and terry cloth robe, she considered how every one of them was lonely and how she was, too, listening to her laundry, alone in a huge city at the edge of the pounding Atlantic Ocean where millions huddled together on a rock piled high with cluttered buildings.

Venus Picatelli, named for *Venus Genetrix*, known as *Anadyomene,* or Rising-from-the-Sea, Aphrodite, a goddess to be welcomed, not feared, originally an obscure Roman deity whose name signified "charm" or "beauty"—scratched her ear, and then scratched her left buttock, and yawned—never realizing that in the very same instant, she was leading a life in your mind.

THE MUSIC OF MIRRORS

Reality invents me;
I am its legend.

Jorge Guillen

A woman lived for a long time without being able to hear anything which was said to her. Her special affliction, it must be understood, was not actual deafness, but something having to do with the look and shape of her face, which was considered to be quite beautiful, and the form of her body which was inviting and voluptuous and pleasing to the eyes of most beholders.

Because this woman was quite beautiful, most people, upon encountering her, would exclaim upon the facts of her physical appeal and completely by-pass or ignore the vibrations she sent out to collect inner sound. Since nearly everyone coming upon her would say: "My Dear, you are beautiful to behold," her senses were soon dulled from hearing the same comment applied over and over again to the fact of her physical existence, and soon, she lost her sense of hearing altogether and became very lonely in a silent world of mirrors.

You see, her world began to consist of nothing but mirrors, and all the people she knew began to turn into mirrors. Their faces slowly melted into flat silver surfaces into which she could gaze and see that what she had heard, over and over again, when she was capable of hearing, was really true. She could look into the shiny flat faces that surrounded her and see that what everyone valued most about her. She could see that what she had heard, over and over again, until her senses were dulled out of existence by repetition, was true.

Unfortunately, the silent world of mirrors which the woman inhabited daily, was an icy world where bedsheets and pillows, spoons and teacups, and hands, themselves, turned into flat cold silent silver surfaces reflecting again and again, the image of her beautiful face.

After many years, as she sat alone, gazing into all the mirrored objects that surrounded her, the woman felt such an unbearable pain of loneliness emanate from all her beautiful reflections that she wept uncontrollably and, in the act of weeping, so distorted her face with the strain of painful loneliness that she noticed she could actually hear. She heard the sound of her own tears falling and her own chest heaving with the gasps of utter sorrow which flowed from her reflections.

At that moment, when she heard her own sobs and realized that she was again hearing, this woman had a marvelous idea which came to her at the exact site of her pituitary gland. She began to let her ears grow. She let them grow until all the curvature and voluptuousness of her body, and all the symmetry and grace of her face flowed into her ears. The rounded smooth breasts which protruded from her chest, the soft red mouth which opened in her head, the firm flesh of her thighs, the curve of her belly, the lovely color of her bright eyes, the exquisite shine of her hair, all, all became concentrated in her ears.

Her ears grew until they were so large and beautiful that her body and face became ugly, guant, and pale. Her entire form so radically changed that people, bit by bit, no longer thought of her as beautiful. They ceased from exclaiming upon the fact of her beauty. They would say things such as: "Oh my poor dear, what tremendous ears you have! What eminent ears; what conspicuous odd gigantic shining ears; what immense ears; what outstandingly prominent ears she has!" they would whisper to each other. "What absurd, out-of-proportion ears she has!" they would gossip, unable to contain themselves. "Oh my God, I've never seen such huge, such hideously big, ears in all my life!" they would emit.

The poor woman who had suffered for so long in her silent world of mirrors found, slowly but surely, as her ears grew and her face and body diminished, that she could hear better than she ever had before. So thrilled was she, in fact, with the music of human speech penetrating what had for such a long time been a silent world, that she did not even notice what in particular was being said, but merely, that sound, lovely sound, was coming from *everything* that existed around her. Then, one day, a person whom the woman had known longer than any other mirror she had ever encountered broke down and blurted: "Oh my God, my pitiful dear, your ears have become so large, and your body so thin, and your face so shriveled, that you have become quite hideous to behold. There must be *something* else about you that I could find to appreciate, because we can no longer remain friends simply upon the basis of your beauty. It is gone. I hate to be cruel, but I can't bear to look at you. It pains me horribly to behold you in such condition. Something must be done! The fact is you are no longer beautiful at all! You are quite disgusting to look at!" He closed his eyes in pity to blot out the image of her face and wept.

The woman, rather than being offended and hurt by his words, was thrilled, for she had heard every word and tear falling so utterly. She was moved deeply by the fact that her world of mirrors had finally been invaded by sound to such a thorough extent. Her sense of hearing had been so miraculously and perfectly restored to her and his voice was so musical and clear and penetrating that his face turned from a mirrored surface into a flesh countenance before her dazzled eyes. So shocked with joy was she to encounter—for the first time in decades—a *flesh* face again, that she gasped and fainted, and fell to the floor, breaking into a thousand pieces, and when the repair men came to put her back together, and hang her upon the wall, her ears would not fit her tiny body. She had to be buried without them and was doomed forever to listen to the loudest silence ever heard by a dead human.

This could be the end of her story, but it would be such a sad place to end that I must go on and tell you what happened next, if for no other reason than the fact that this should not be the end of any woman's story:

As the poor woman lay cold beneath the ground listening to the loudest silence ever heard by a dead person, something wonderful began to happen. Very slowly, from the place where her heart moldered in agony a leaf began to grow, an exquisite leaf which after a long time of growing became a tree—a tree so beautiful and fragrant, invitingly comfortable, peaceful and silent, standing in the sun and quietly photosynthesizing light into the matter of its being, that millions of song birds came to live contentedly in its tempting, sheltering branches to sing uncontrollably. They sang so sweetly and so beautifully and with such grace and absolute precision, for so happy were they to be in the branches of this tree, that their song was ecstasy, the very sound of ecstasy itself, a sound so thrillingly penetrating that it vibrated through the entire tree and down into the roots which grew above the dead woman's heart.

The roots vibrated and shimmered with the sounds of millions of birds singing, and so much so that they began to shift position beneath the earth and swim about under the soil as if in a dance of ecstasy. One root vibrated and slipped into the woman's silent mouth; another shimmered into her vagina and another wriggled into her uterus. In fact, the birds sang so fully and exquisitely every melody that was or had ever been that each nook and cranny, every crevice of orifice, of the woman's body and bones, every dead cell of her, became filled with roots.

Roots as thin as capillaries and roots as large as a wrist filled her and wriggled inside of her, vibrating in her corpse so that she was no longer distinguishable from the matter of the tree with the singing birds in its branches. She vibrated with sound. She heard the very sound of sheer ectasy move within her womb. Sound filled her and sound became the essence of her. Her body was music—the music of ecstasy itself. The dead woman became pregnant with sound, filled with the poetry of music, bloated with the ecstasy of song and was doomed forever to listening to the beauty which had once been her face.

DAFFODIL DOLLARS

The immediate beauty of a rag in the wind...
The immense stone statue of a grain of salt.
The joy of every day and the uncertainty of dying
and the iron of love in the wound of a smile.

Jacques Prevert

"Grass so green it sticks to my tongue, flowers too bright hurt my eyes. His eyes don't want me now. Fell asleep snoring without needing me all week. Tomorrow and tomorrow and tomorrow creeps in this petty pace.... His snores bore me. Spring beginning so wet, pink, purple, everywhere, damp, bright green creeps in this petty pace from day to day 'til the last syllable of recorded time and all our yesterdays have lighted fools the way to nuclear dust. A woman can never play Hamlet, Macbeth, or Lear, anyway. She plays *A Doll's House*, *Anna Karenina*, or *Madame Bovary*. Maybe St. Joan burning in self-sacrifice. I should jump and then he'd be sorry to see me in the river of recorded time, black and blue and swollen like a dead fish, this body he used to call love, like a morning glory, blue and drowned purple. If I could, would they be sorry then to see me, tomorrow and tomorrow creeps. No one understands my raw heart, voice like a violet hunger, dark blue lips, tiny blossoms of tits. My best performance. If the critics neglect this one, I might as well be dead. Ophelia floats, crazy and gone. He doesn't touch me; must be another woman somewhere. I'm dead like Daddy now, under the violets, mouth stopped with dust. The green grass sticks to my tongue, I want to vomit. I can't eat, getting anorexic, thin." An actress thinks as she collapses on a bench of Cherry Blossom

Lane in The Brooklyn Botanic Gardens.

Plush pink blossoms surround her in her flowery blue dress. A riot of pink blossoms and vibrant color glows amidst the new April rinsed, May greenery. She looks down at her delicate, manicured hands. They flop like dead birds in her lap. She looks down at the newspaper beneath them, the drama section of *The New York Times*. She is weary of playing secondary roles in classic dramas. At the age of thirty, though she is considered by her colleagues to be an extraordinary actress, she has not achieved much recognition. She just opened in a Broadway revival and the reviewers have failed, once again, to hail her talent with great plaudits. Praise went to all the big name stars who overshadowed her.

She imagines herself lying flat on her back, dead beneath the bench where she sits. Some children play in the grass of the public gardens, gamboling happily. After a while, the actress notices a dwarf woman hobbling slowly toward her beneath the canopy of pink blossoms along the path. The dwarf is extremely short and elephantine legs seem sore with the stress of carrying her nearly normal-sized trunk and head. The old dwarf approaches the lovely blond actress who stares at her in a daze.

"Good morning!" The dwarf smiles cheerfully despite the pain in her grotesquely short legs. When the pretty woman doesn't answer, the dwarf's smile intensifies. "Beautiful morning; isn't it?"

A little afraid of staring at the small lame woman—and unaware she has been doing so—the woman answers with a forced smile, "...Yes."

The dwarf is undaunted. "Really beautiful? Really absolutely gorgeous, isn't it?"

Finally, the actress concedes without drama, "Yes, lovely."

Using the young woman's answer as an excuse for coming even nearer, the dwarf embellishes, "Lovely; yes, lovely. You are lovely, too, I see. Like this spring morning. A beautiful woman surrounded by cherry blossoms. What a wonderful sight."

The woman, always embarrassed by compliments, but wanting to be gracious, managed to say, "Thank you. That's very kind of you." She feels extremely awkward as the dwarf continues smiling directly into her eyes—enough so that the actress can smell coffee on her breath. "This is the nicest morning we've had since the end of winter. Mind if I share this bench with you for a moment? My legs start aching after I've made it half way around the gardens, so, I take a rest."

The young woman doesn't know what to say. "That's too bad," but though she expresses empathy, she does not move aside to welcome the dwarf.

The small woman becomes wary. "Well, I could sit way over there on that other bench, but..."

Suddenly cognizant of her oversight, the actress is quick to correct it. "Oh, no. I'm sorry. This is fine. There's plenty of room here."

"Good, then, if you really don't mind. I just feel like I can't go another step just now. Not without a little rest."

There is an awkward silence in which the dwarf struggles to seat herself on the bench and the normal woman is not sure whether to offer assistance.

"May I help you up?"

"No, no. That's okay, deary. I can make it by myself. Always have. Always will. It just takes me a little longer, but I'm never in a hurry anyway. No place to hurry to. These benches aren't quite my size, ya know."

There's another silence in which the normal woman doesn't know what to say. After the dwarf is comfortably seated, the woman opens her paper. As she tries to read, the dwarf watches her closely. The woman's mind wanders to a sparrow, some children singing, the sun through the trees. Finally, she replays in her mind the dwarf's painful approach along the path beneath the cherry blossoms.

Suddenly, the dwarf interrupts the silence as if reading her mind. she leans closer to the actress as she speaks. "All my brothers and sisters were normal, ya know. I was the only one born with short legs and arms. The rest of the family was very tall, nice looking, normal-sized."

Again, the actress doesn't know how to respond. She nods and then returns to her newspaper.

After a short silence, the dwarf adds, "But, I'm healthy. I've got my health. I'm lucky to have that. It's only my legs that bother me. Otherwise, I'm in perfect health. I thank God for that."

"That's good. Health is the most important thing." The actress gives up her reading.

"Yes, more important than anything else. And, I'd rather have short legs than be blind, for example. I can see the flowers. Enjoy the spring—like everybody else. I feel glad to be alive on a gorgeous day like this; don't you?"

Nodding and smiling, the actress agrees. She begins to watch the dwarf intently. "I'm not sure I have the spirit that you do for spring or anything else."

"What are you reading?"

"A theatrical review... in the *Times*. I was...I ..."

"Ah, the theatre. I love the theatre, too." When the actress doesn't respond, she questions, "What do you do? Are you an actress? You look pretty enough to be one of them movie stars."

"Thank you. Yes, I'm an actress, a stage actress, but I've only played secondary roles...."

"Oh my, an actress. How wonderful. A pretty girl like you, and an actress, too. That's nice." The dwarf pauses and smiles broadly. "Look at the children playing. It's such a beautiful day. I'm glad to be alive on a day like this. I've got my own room, ya know. With a refrigerator and a stove and everything. I have to use the bathroom in the hall. It could use some paint, but at least it's clean. The superintendent keeps it nice and clean. I live right over there on Eastern Parkway. Right across from the gardens—in a rent controlled building. The landlord might sell though, for co-oping. That's my only worry. I take a walk in the gardens most every day when it's nice like this. The cherry blossoms are beautiful, but the rain washed some of them off on Tuesday. That heavy rain we had? They're best when it doesn't rain just after they bloom, ya know. I like acting, too, ya know, and poetry, too. I have a poem right here in my head." She points to her oversized cranium. "I like to say it this time of the year, especially. It's a wonderful poem for springtime." She struggles down from the bench and takes a theatrical stance in front of the woman. "Would you like to hear it?"

"All right...I mean, yes, I'd like to hear it..." She can hardly refuse.

"Good. It goes like this: "I wandered lonely as a cloud/ That floats on high o'er vales and hills/ When all at once I saw a crowd,/ A host, of golden daffodils..." She continues very slowly and dramatically, reciting and gesturing in a corny, but charming way, Wordsworth's hackneyed poem "Daffodils."

The woman tries to listen patiently and

attentively, but her mind wanders to a tree, some flowers, a bird chirping, a sun beam through the blossoms, and finally, returns to the dwarf's brimming eyes. Chopin's *Fantasy Impromptu* plays in the recesses of her mind as she notices her own hands lying limply in her lap, and then focuses on the dwarf's hand gesturing in air.

"I gazed and gazed, but little thought, What wealth to me the show had brought:/ For oft, when on my couch I lie/ in vacant or in pensive mood,/ They flash upon that inward eye/ Which is the bliss of solitudes/ And then my heart with pleasure fills,/ And dances with the daffodils." The dwarf concludes with a tiny leap, suggestive of a dance, then curtsies as best she can, tottering on her small legs.

The young woman feels compelled to clap and say: "It's a lovely poem and you say it very nicely."

"I think I might have been an actress if life had been a little different to me." She comes closer to confide. "But, I'm not complaining, ya know. I've got my health and I've got my room, right near these beautiful public gardens, and all. No sin! I'm not complaining."

"You've got a great spirit." The actress is sincere. "I know lots of people in much better circumstances who don't have the courage you have. You're fortunate to have such peace of mind."

"Well, like I always say, I could be worse off...and I can see the flowers. Have you seen the little spice garden here? It's really nice. It's over there next to the Japanese Garden. They have these little Braille plaques so that the blind can read those little bumpy dots to know which spice or herb they are smelling. It's nice there. The ledge where they plant the spices and herbs is just the right height for me. I don't have to bend down like other people in order to smell the plants. The spices grow right at my nose." She laughs heartily. "I like to smell the mint best, and the basil and bay leaves. They smell so clean and fresh, especially right after the rain, ya know. I'm tempted to pick some of that mint for my tea, and those bay leaves for my soup, but I don't. It wouldn't be nice. It's for the blind and all...Well, I better be getting along. You probably want to finish reading your newspaper. Did you really like that poem I recited for you?

The woman, feeling calmer than she has, responds warmly. "Thank you...very much. It's been nice talking with you."

The dwarf's tone abruptly changes. She speaks rapidly. "Well, I have copies of that poem right here for only one dollar. Typed 'em myself." She puts her hand in her bag and pulls out a stack of papers. "Here they are. Would you like to have one; only one dollar." She thrusts a page into the woman's hands. "I charge only one dollar even though it takes me a long time to type them. My fingers aren't so good these days, ya know."

The young woman, taken off guard by the dwarf's excellent salesmanship, can't refuse. She rummages in her purse for some money. As she does so, the dwarf asks: "Do you like this hat I'm wearing? Do you?"

"Yes, I...."

"I made it myself. Crocheted it. Do you really like it?"

"Yes...It's very nice."

"Only five dollars. I have a green one and a red one." The dwarf pulls out two hats like the one she is wearing. She places the green one on the young woman's head before the seated woman can protest. "See. Fits you perfectly! Looks good on you. Perfect! Looks real nice on you. Better than on me 'cause you're better looking!" She laughs heartily. "Only five dollars. Handmade. That will be six dollars with the poem."

As if hypnotized, the actress hands the dwarf six dollars. The money lies across the dwarf's palm for what seems to the young woman an eternity. Chopin's *Fantasy Impromptu* plays again in the recesses of her skull. Then she looks at the dwarf's eyes, but they seem to have dollar bills pasted over them. For an instant the woman imagines her own face with dollar bills pasted over it. The dwarf stuffs the money into the bodice of her dress which the woman notices, for the first time, is printed with tiny golden daffodils. "Thanks, deary. Bye."

The young woman watches the small lame woman exit down the path beneath the plush canopy of spring blossoms, limping, it seems, not quite as severely as she had appeared to upon approaching. She notices a sunbeam flicker over the dwarf's head; a sparrow flits to another branch; some children laughing in a game of catch; a cherry blossom fallen in her lap.

MRS. PRISM'S FIRST DEATH

The future of religion is in the mystery of touch.
D.H. Lawrence

The grandfather clock in the hallway struck the hour and began to chime: One. Two. Three. Four. Five. Six. Seven. Eight. Nine. Ten. Eleven. The fringe on the lampshade jiggled as she got up from her chair to smooth her dress and her hair, always done up in the same neat coiffure.

She pushed the lace curtain aside and peered out onto East 70th Street where the snow had begun again to fall lightly. A Model-T Ford made its way down the street, the chains on its wheels chiming against the shoveled macadam like a grandfather clock far off in the distance. Headlights flickered across the dim ceiling and across Mrs. Prism's face.

Shivering from the cold at the windowpane, she took a long look at the flakes dancing in the glow of the streetlamps, and then opened the window just enough to scrape a handful of snow from the windowsill. She looked behind her to make sure no one was watching and then licked the snow from her palm. She couldn't let the children see her eating snow, because she was always careful to tell them not to put snow into their mouths. "Heaven knows what sort of dirt might be in it," the children's nurse always told them, "especially in a city like this!"

Mrs. Prism had lived in the brownstone house on East 70th Street for all the eight years of her married life, and she had lived there for the three years since her husband's death—coming and going in her black mourning clothes which she wore constantly, not so much out of continuing sorrow, but as an excuse to remain quiet and aloof from society. The few people who knew her believed her to be resolvedly and relentlessly mourning her husband's death, and, she allowed them to think just that—always letting as few words as possible escape her lips. For three winters she had sat by the fire, knitting sweater after scarf, mitten after mitten, for her three children—two daughters and one son who was the oldest and now nine.

Mrs. Prism had married Mr. Prism when she was eighteen years old and they had had three children. A respectable financeer and banker, he had left just enough money behind for his family to live in moderate comfort. All in all, Mrs. Prism had a very neat and scheduled life—not enough money to spend lavishly, but enough to live out her life, if she was careful and frugal, which, of course, she was: knitting and sewing her own clothes and the children's, and canning and baking and caring for the house without the help of servants. Her only luxury was the children's nurse, whom she wouldn't have employed except for the fact that her nerves were not so good and she couldn't bear to be with them every minute of the day tending to their little childlike whines and whinnies.

She liked to get away to her secluded bedroom on the second floor and cozy up under her big magenta feather comforter and read novel after novel, most of which she kept carefully hidden from the children—because of their prurient nature, she told herself. It had taken her quite some effort to forgive Dostoievsky, Tolstoy, Thomas Hardy, George Eliot, Charlotte Bronte, Balzac, Flaubert, Edith Wharton, or Theodore Dreiser, for their trespasses into the world of incontinent interests, but she had managed to do so, eventually. Still, these were not books for the eyes of young Alfred, now nearly ten years old and beginning to be curious about such things. She left all of Alfred's questions to his nurse's indiscretion. She also avoided his bathtime, because his growing body had begun to make her feel uneasy.

Every day, just after lunch, Mrs. Prism climbed the stairs to her room and locked her door behind her. She took whatever book she was reading from the locked chest where she kept her novels. Then, removing her black skirt and two white petticoats (so as not to wrinkle them) and, taking off her bloomers (just to be more comfortable), she climbed into bed, arranged herself among the big feather pillows, pulled the soft magenta comforter over her naked legs, and settled down to read for two or more hours—sometimes falling into a light sleep in which she imagined herself to be Natasha conversing with Prince Myshkin; Matty dining with Ethan; Tess wandering with her empty milk pail in a sun-soaked field of daisies; or Catherine searching in a ghost-like trance through the moorland for her lost and loving Heathcliff.

Her bare legs would tingle and her groin ache a little under the warm comforters with the pleasure of romance and the thrill of drama conjured up in her by her reading, but never ever once did it occur to Mrs. Prism that she might slide a hand beneath her comforter to relieve the tension built up in her thighs, traveling up through her spinal cord, knotting the base of her neck until her head felt as brittle as a china teacup. Such an idea was quite beyond her understanding. At one time or another, she, perhaps, heard that young men do such things during adolescence, but she did not even know that masturbation was possible in the domain of women. She was quite unaware of the potential for pleasure in the tiny organ of her own body and its name was not even a part of her vocabulary.

It was Mr. Prism who had wanted the children, not she. She couldn't bear the thought of what would have to transpire between them to make a child, but, she had submitted dutifully to her husband—enough to make three children during the eight years of their marriage. Then, one day, Mr. Prism accidentally stepped in front of a trolley and was gone from her life as quickly as he had entered it.

She never really wanted to marry him, and secretly with a desperate guilt, was glad that he was gone. He hurt her so that first night with his moist rough hands and clumsy insistence, silently climbing over her trembling body and pressing himself into her without a word—pushing just enough to hurt. Then he'd be done and would roll over and fall quickly into sleep, leaving her aching and ashamed. Yes, she was glad he was gone, even if the guilt of her gladness choked her like a fish bone caught in her windpipe.

"He'll make a fine husband and a good father and provider!" her mother had said. "You'll be taken care of and your poor old mother won't have to worry about you. You'd better say 'yes,' Abbey! You can't think about silly ideas of love and romance at a time like this. Every woman needs a husband to take care of her, and who knows when you'll get a chance to marry a man as solid as Henry Prism again!" her mother had warned. "It's much better than having to look for the sort of a job a woman can get, typing or sewing all day in this dreadful city."

Mrs. Prism was so tentative and shy that she barely had a friend in the world before marrying Mr. Prism. Her father was a strong-willed Presbyterian minister sent down from Massachusettes to take over a New York parish. Mrs. Prism had gone to the

Presbyterian school within her father's dominion and had been careful to set a good example for her fellow students. "Always make me proud of you, Abbey. Carry yourself like a lady and a woman of God!" her father said over and over, drumming the words into her head. She hardly dared make a move for fear of doing some thing that would be considered improper by her father's parishoners. It was easier to be timid and not speak up, to be sweet and just nod and smile all the time and not let anyone know what nasty thoughts you might be thinking.

An only child, she was devoted to her parents, fetching and carrying for them right up until the day of her father's death. A year later, she married Mr. Prism, and her mother went back to Massachusetts to live with her maiden sister on the small pension provided by the church. So, there was Mrs. Prism, when her husband died, all alone in the big city with her three children. She kept the nurse her husband had hired to take charge of the children when he realized how nervous she was after the difficult birth of their son.

But, Mrs. Prism was attractive. She wore her long blond hair in a knot on the top of her head and her wide eyes were a deep blue. Though her skin was too pale, it was clear and her lips were delicately full. She was, however, absolutely incapable of talking to anyone but the members of her own family. She shook when she tried to speak to strangers. Sweat formed on her brow. Her lips twitched, and her eyes blinked until she had to close them. This condition became so pro-nounced after her husband's death that the nurse had to do all the shopping and marketing. Mrs. Prism couldn't even get a word out to the clerks in the stores.

She reflected for a moment on how this always happened to her and how terribly humiliating it was.

She pressed her forehead to the windowpane letting the coldness of it numb her aching head. She saw herself lying face down in the snow under the chains on the wheels of a Model-T Ford crushing her face into the snow and macadam. She thought of what happened earlier that evening at the home of her sister-in-law, Sarah, who had invited her to dinner. Sarah had also invited a pianist who lived in the neighborhood to meet Mrs. Prism, but when the musician turned to her to talk about his trip to Paris and asked if she'd ever been there, it happened as it always did. It was a simple question. All she had to say was: "No, I haven't," but she couldn't. Her body began to shake; her eyes twitched; her face got hot and she couldn't speak a word. She pretended to choke on her chocolate mousse. And he, somehow feeling her embarrassment, just talked on to the others as if nothing at all had happened. She wondered if he was just being kind because he thought she was a spastic or an epileptic or something. It was so humiliating! She'd seen this man many times passing her on the street where they both lived. He always tipped his hat and gave a pleasant greeting to which she simply nodded. They had been introduced for the first time that evening by her sister-in-law, Sarah, who lived around the corner .

Because Sarah had decided, at this late date in her life, and to everyone's amazement to learn to play the piano, the musician had recently become her piano teacher. "To keep my mind off my ailments," she'd said. She tried to convince Mrs. Prism to take lessons too: "It will be good for you, Abbey! You'll get your mind off my poor brother's untimely passing. You can use my piano whenever you wish to practice. It will cost very little extra if we take the lessons together. Harold won't mind if I pay for the both of us. Give it a try."

Mrs. Prism answered that she'd think about it, but she knew she wouldn't. How could she learn to play in front of a stranger whose presence would make her hands tremble horribly all the while? Sarah meant to introduce her to the musician that evening to make her more comfortable about trying the lessons, but it was no use. She'd excused herself immediately after dinner, with her few words directed toward Sarah, with whom she had managed some conversation over years of trying. To the pianist she could only utter a quiet "Good-night," after which she hurried home to sit by the fire and knit.

She had been knitting furiously until the clock struck eleven. Then she'd looked out the window at the snow, tasted the cool snow on her warm tongue and felt its cool wetness in her hand where it melted and disappeared in her fist.

She opened the window again to reach for another fistful of snow and heard a bell ringing, or thought she did. Startled by the sound, she looked out on the street; everything stood quiet in the snow. Then, she was jarred into the realization that it was her own telephone ringing in the hall. She'd heard the sound of its ring quite seldom since her husband's death, and certainly, never at this hour of the night. Her sister-in-law, one of the very few people who ever phoned her, was ailing and always in bed before eleven. Mrs. Prism couldn't imagine that anyone would be calling her at such a late hour, and so, she went to the telephone to inform the party calling that they must have the wrong number. A thick voice, when she lifted the receiver, said, "Good evening. Is this the beautiful shy Mrs. Prism?"

For a moment she couldn't believe that the voice was asking for her. Indeed, she almost forgot her name. Could someone be calling her and at this hour? Her voice failed her and she began to stutter as she always did. "Whoo oo is is isis th th th this?" she asked, but the moment she asked, she knew. It was the piano teacher she met at Sarah's earlier in the evening. She knew it was he. She could see his dark, piercing eyes as if he were there in the hall with her. She pulled her collar tight about her neck as the voice continued.

"Is this the beautiful Mrs. Prism?" he said again. "You are such a lovely lady; you should not be afraid to speak. Speak, and tell me, please, if it is you," he said.

There was a long silence; she could hear him sigh and breathe.

"Come now, Mrs. Prism, don't be afraid. Is it you?"

"Yeh yeh yes," she finally heard her dry voice come out of her throat, though it didn't sound like her voice at all. "It it it issss me. HHHow dare you ca ca call me at this hour, Si Si Sir!" she managed quickly with less stammering because her anger and the insult were now clear.

"But, my dear lady, I thought that I was speaking to a beautiful woman and a lady, not a shop girl! Please, My Dear Lady, if you are a lady and not a silly shop-girl, I would love to have you come across the way to my apartment to join me for a drink. I just saw you at your window. It would be good of you to join me for a drink. Please do come over. I live as you may know on the first floor across the way from you. Number one-seventy-one. I will be waiting patiently and will accept you and expect you at whatever moment you arrive with great cordiality and pleasure. I know that you are a lovely woman and not a silly shop girl. Remember I will be waiting patiently for you to come."

There was a click and the receiver was silent.

Mrs. Prism stood in the hall for a full seven minutes with the telephone still pressed to her ear, shivering and shaking and perspiring. Then she realized what she was doing and quickly clamped the receiver down as if an obscene word had just come out of it. She rubbed her hands together and rubbed her cheeks. She took her handkerchief from her pocket and blotted her brow. She paced back and forth in the hall. Ten minutes went by.

She went into the parlor, very conscious now of the windows, and picked up her knitting. She sat staring into the fire; its flames were burning low and the last of two logs crackled with orange embers. She saw the red light of the fire at its edges and the bright orange and yellow and blue and violet in its flames. She saw the white glow around it. The fire burned deeply into the sockets of her eyes. If anyone had been there in the silent room with her, it would have seemed to them that the fire had transferred itself to Mrs. Prism's eyes and was burning with tiny flames in the mirrors of her pupils.

She sat staring into the fire, flames dancing in her eyes, for a full eighteen minutes, as if hypnotized. Then she went swiftly to the back of the house, her heels clicking quietly through the hall. She opened the door of her daughters' room. A streak of light fell across the twin beds of the little girls and she could see their chests rising and falling softly in the deepness of sleep. She closed the door quietly and walked to the other side of the hall. She carefully opened the door to her son's room where a tiny light was always kept burning against his fear of being alone in the dark. He was soundly asleep, breathing softly. She went to the end of the corridor. She looked for a light under the nurse's door. There was none. She put her ear to the door. She could hear Alice's muffled steady snore .

Turning quickly around, she went to the hall closet and grabbed her coat from its hanger so that the hanger was left swinging on the closet pole. She shoved her arms into the smooth satin lining. She took her boots from the floor and pulled them quickly over her shoes. A scarf, one she had knitted herself, of course, went quickly around her neck. She turned and caught sight of herself in the hall mirror. She was wearing a strange smile—a sort of smile she had never seen on her own face, one she had never imagined crossing her lips. She went up close to the mirror and peered at her pale face. A wisp of blond hair had fallen over her brow. She lifted her hand to smooth it into place, but her hand changed its mind in mid air and pulled the wisp lower over her eye. The strange smile remained on her face, but now she was not sure it was her face at all for she could not make the smile leave her lips. It was the face of some stranger inhabiting her skin. The smile frightened her. She looked away. She went back to the closet and took off her coat and hung it on the hanger which still swung gently on the pole. Her coat was hanging there before her. Ten more minutes passed as she stood staring at it, noticing the way the arms curved as if her arms were still in them, the way the bodice puffed out where her breasts fit into it. It was as if she were hanging there in the closet, hanging headless from a pole.

". . . his voice a magenta comforter. . . his eyes feather pillows. . . hands that play the piano. . . Henry

Prism rotted now. . . the body he forced into me. . . dust.
. . like the ashes of the fire. . . the smell of wool. . . dust
like the dust in snow. . . Myshkin only Myshkin could
have saved her. . . I'm gone into coldness . . . my skin. .
. naked. . . won't be young longer. . . his clumsy hands
and the doctor's. . . pain of children. . . legs opened and
eyes blinded by tidal waves. . . rushing over my face. . .
tongue drowning . . . can't speak. . . floating away. . .
brain melting. . . choking on my father and his god and
the pain of opening to let them in and let them out. . .
husband words father and children. . . always cleaning
all the dust. . . the dust of Henry and the dust of father
. . . the dust of God. . . tongue dry with the dust of the
pain of opening to let them in and let them out. . .
husband words and children. . . close the clothes the
close the closet. . ."

She yanked herself from the hanger. The
wooden hanger fell to the floor with a thud. She froze,
listening for a noise from the end of the hall, but the
house was silent, except that the clock behind her began
chiming and she fell back against the open closet door.
It seemed to her that her heart was beating twenty beats
to every chime of the old grandfather clock. One. Two.
Three. Four. Five. Six. Seven. Eight. Nine. Ten.
Quickly, she was out the door and the latch clicked
behind her. The last two chimes of the clock sounded
faintly behind the etched glass of the door: Eleven.
Twelve, midnight. Hurriedly, she crossed the snow
blanketed street leaving dainty tracks behind her. No
cars had passed for an hour. "There is not a crease in the
new white snow," she thought, but she wasn't really
thinking at all. She had stopped thinking and was
merely moving up the stairs of the house numbered:

one-seventy-one. She saw her hand as if disembodied take hold of the door knocker in front of her, and the door swing open as if by magic before she could tap the knocker even once. Her hand jumped back. "Good evening, Mrs. Prism, " he said in his thick deep voice and she saw his eyes, just as she remembered them, staring out from the dim light of the foyer. I was waiting at the window, because I wanted so much for you to come. I saw you leave your front door. I've waited for almost an hour, hoping you'd come. "Please let me take your coat, Dear Lady. And do come in and sit down. I have some brandy waiting for us by the fire. Come, Dear Lady! You are even more beautiful with your blond hair over your eye. "

Mrs. Prism wondered if her face still wore that strange smile. She wasn't sure, because her face as she knew it, was completely out of control. She had no way of knowing or imagining what it must look like to this man who spoke so directly and easily and with such relaxation in his throat.

She knew that her body was trembling, or that the body she stood in was trembling and she couldn't open her mouth. She let him lead her by the elbow over to the fire and seat her in an armchair.

"You are a lovely woman, My Dear, and I understand your fear, but you musn't be afraid of me. I want to be the first real friend you have had." He was kneeling before her and gently removing her boots. His steady light hands gripped her ankle and slid her boot, like a loose glove, from her shoe.

"I am thrilled by the prospect of a friendship with as lovely and delicate a lady as you. Your silence is quite beautiful and I understand it very well, " he said. "It is the silence of a bird who can sing too well for the shabby forest in which it finds itself. It is the silence of a golden fish, who can only breathe water, caught gasping on land for air. He spoke softly as he handed her a glass and she automatically sipped from it. It was easier than trying to talk for a moment, and weren't his words absolving her from talk? Couldn't she sit there with him in silence and wouldn't he understand?

He was saying something that showed he understood. He sat in an armchair across from her. He was silent too. He sat there in the silence of the room and watched the fire light play over her face as she watched her hands holding her glass.

Somewhere in a dark green jungle, beyond the literary cliche of eating oranges, a ripe orange is being eaten. Hands curl around its globe; fingernails dig into the spongy skin and tear it from the moist fruit. A squirt of juice escapes a hole made in the sweet flesh. Fingers pull one section from another, separate one soft labia from another, to make an opening--peeling skin from skin. Fingers, more actual than Freudian, press into a moist opening: a slit from which juice oozes more freely than from a D. H. Lawrence fig, more freely than from the orange in your mind as you read this. A thing is separated from itself: a living body, once whole, oozes from its being. A mouth like a cave of death takes it in. Teeth mash its juice from it. If it could think, and who knows for sure that it doesn't, it would think of itself swimming in its own life's blood. It would feel itself squashed within the walls of a stomach, churned to pulp, digested and become one with its eater, become its eater's flesh and blood. More profoundly than fresh oil stain sinks into unfinished wood, as certainly as dye penetrates cotton, as completely as hydrogen mixes with oxygen to become water, the orange knows it is a part of the living animal, crouched in the darkness eating. Llife is feeling and God is in the blood and

*blood is in the mind coursing through the brain of it.
There is no pure thought, no real abstraction, only
chemical formulas of the blood of which we are all a
part in the body of God even when he is smeared on the
hands of the murderer, the hairy hand of death that
plucks fruit from a tree in a dark green jungle. And the
cave of death which is the mouth of God, become the
womb of thought, full of breath and moist tongue, gives
birth to the word.*

  After several minutes passed, Mrs. Prism
raised her eyes to his face. They sat there for more than
an hour, looking across the five feet of carpet that
separated their chairs into each other's eyes, saying
more than if they had spoken. Mrs. Prism began to feel
her body stop trembling and her eyes were not blinking
anymore. And, just at the moment when she began to
feel as comfortable as if she were sitting in front of her
own fire knitting, he spoke once again, his voice more
relaxed and thicker than ever: "You are so lovely, My
Dear, and there is nothing to be afraid of. I want to be
very gentle with you, as gentle as I would be with a
small wounded bird. You are a wounded bird and the
bones of your heart are so fragile, like the high notes of
the piano played in a Chopin Nocturne. I could not hurt
you at all. I want only to make you happy and
comfortable," he said as he rose from his chair and came
toward her .

  She was climbing the stairs with him. His hand
was around her waist. Then she felt him sweep her into
his arms and she was being carried across the landing
into a room that was dark except for the glow of a street
lamp in the window. He laid her gently down on the bed
and kissed her forehead. She felt nothing at all except
his lips. Her body seemed to be gone from her. She felt
as light as if she were flying or dangling from a web. He

left her for a moment and when he returned his arms and chest were naked. She couldn't bring herself to look at the rest of him. He leaned over her again and this time he kissed her throat and whispered softly into her ear that she was beautiful and that he had wanted her for a long time. He said that he had wanted her when he saw her passing in the street and when he saw her at her sister-in-law's earlier in the evening.

"You are lovely and gentle and I will not hurt you at all. " he said through his breath.

His hands were rustling the buttons of her blouse: One. Two. Three. Four. Five. Six. Seven buttons were opened as if a clock were chiming, as if they were climbing the stairs. She felt the cool air against her neck and throat. She felt his mouth pressed where the cool air had entered her blouse.

Then his mouth was on her mouth and his hands were on her breasts, his fingers touching her nipples. She must have fainted or blanked out because she couldn't remember for a moment how she got there. Some time must have passed--time spent only in mindless sensation. She lay there under his warm body and his mouth was in her hair, caressing her ear. His hands held her shoulders and then her breasts. His body was moving rhythmically over hers. Her skirt was gone and her petticoats and her underwear, and she was not trembling.

"You are exquisite, a rare exquisite bird, " he was whispering. "I want to make your body sing for me as it has never sung for anyone. My Sweet Virgin Madonna. I want to make your body sing for me as it has never sung before."

His head was between her legs. His tongue was licking her. She was near to fainting again. She tried to realize that she was there with him, that his hands were on her nipples, gently rubbing across them, that his face was buried in the part of her she tried never to think of at all. His tongue was licking her. One. Two. Three. Four. Five. Six. Seven. Eight. Nine. Ten. Eleven. Twelve.... strokes, as if a clock were chiming, as if she were climbing the stairs, as if she were reading Dostoievsky under her feather comforter and she were Natasha being murdered. She began to feel a weakness come over her. She couldn't believe that he was doing such a thing to her, but a weakness began to well up from her knees as if the life were flowing over and out of her and she leapt up from the bed and ran to the window and screamed: "I'm dying, l'm dying; the life is flowing out of me!" and the words came out *perfectly* clear.

MARITAL BLISS

Psychology which explains everything
explains nothing and we are still in doubt.
Marianne Moore

The secret of life sang in Pete's pants to be mismderstood and forgotten. He was a womanizer whose ethnos no one knew—not even himself—because he was entirely American. Mary Alice his wife had never touched with the dumb fury of tongues or drawn a moan of ecstasy from the bent world's insanity. If Mary Alice and Pete could have spoken to each other with their thighs and thought with their hands, they might have made sweet music against the belly of eternity or sang the algebra of glands to the wet mathematics of creation as if God lived in our bodies and we prayed to them with the dreams of our fingers. Pete had big blue eyes and muscles and a huge double barreled shotgun, easily unzipped and fired anywhere. He went all around the town aiming it at every woman he could, then carving commemorative notches on his leather belt with his sleek and steely penknife. He walked down the street flashing his groin, hips and chest and elbows moving in the fresh air. His animal nature billowed along with him so that even those angered by it were charmed, as had been Mary Alice long ago. She was pretty, but plain compared to Pete.

"I am a man," Pete thought.

"No, you're not," whispered his wife, Mary Alice, who stayed home caring for all the children he'd fathered in the house and on the lawn and in the garage, and in the back seat of his old souped-up Plymouth, and all around the neighborhood and the city. She kept them all tucked up under her tattered skirts, safe from the cold and want which was their lot. She even started a day-care center to give them friends to play with and to earn money for all the rare hamburgers and cold beers Pete thrived on to consummate his consuming.

But, the Mayor and City Hall closed Mary Alice's Day Care Center, because she naively didn't have a degree or a license, so, she started a home laundry and all the kids pitched in, hanging out the clothes, because she made a cheery game of it—singing nursery rhymes while they worked—about a maid in the garden hanging out the Clothes a snippy Blackbird, and a king with alot of birds baked into his fat pie.

She managed pretty well and kept handsome Pete in hamburgers, too.

"This is a good life, " Pete said, until he grew older and his shotgun rusted and became bent from so much firing—as bent as the famous one in the limerick about the young man from Kent who instead of coming, went.

So Mary Alice, who had a pleasant matronly face, to save his male pride, since she'd become, by feverish work, the most important laundress in the whole town, set him to work driving her laundry truck, to keep his mind off his problem, and keep him going.

"We don't talk much, Pete," she pointed out one day.

"Huh?" asked Pete? watching the final playoff of the World Serious on T.V, "Talk? About what?"

"Well, maybe our children, for example."

"Oh, them? They're kinda cute—especially the little girls—the way they hop and skip and call me 'Daddy' and look up to me."

"Well, "said Mary Alice. "You are a lot taller."

One friday, as Pete was driving Mary Alice

along in the truck on their way to deposit a month's laundry earnings in the bank, they were held up at a red light by a guy with a little tiny revolver which he pointed stiffly at Alice's breast. Alice, clutching her purse, full of money, to her chest with her reddened knuckles, pretended to faint, and that gave Pete who had alot of confidence from all the notches in his leather belt, time to rip it off and lash the hairy wrist holding the tiny revolver with it, using it like a lion tamer's whip.

Then, Pete knocked the robber down, as the robber dropped his gun and Pete his pants. Pete sat on the robber while Mary Alice ran for the police.

Later, that evening, Mary Alice and Pete drove home together and shut out the lights—after all the children were tucked in—and Pete made love for the first time in his life to anyone, to Mary Alice, his wife, because he thought how scared he'd be without her when the robber pointed his revolver at her breast and threatened to shoot her dead. He thought of her as a small furry animal, warm and soft with a dark hold of worry in the center of her—wet and inviting—a place he could fill with himself. She felt like the object of his need, pressed between her thighs waiting to be opened by touch. His fingers willed the thrill of her desire and a warm light exploded a sunburst in their dark minds. Her face shed the winter of its worry over all the murdered roses torn from flesh with tortured shrieks. Her skin bloomed like spring petals, pitying and pink, yellow, purple veined buds of beneficent being filled her dreams and Pete's red heart burned him with her life and she understood, for the first time, all the life, like an indigestible summer of merciless heat, she had pushed out of herself, She heard Pete's sweet murmurs in the night and thought of how hard and selfish he could be and pulled herself closer, and he rubbed her back and neck, and she felt him become the father of all things waiting to be spilled into and out of her, to make her bloom like a round melon. She understood why the roses must die to be beautiful like the sea from which she smelled her own body, throbbing and rolling as he thrust need into her. She felt as necessary as earth planted in spring so that grass grows for eating, vibrant in the green summer sun, festering with insects, birds, sticky throated

flowers. Syllables spilled prattling to the small round animals that came seeing out of her, breathing her belly—laughing, weeping, seeping, whelping, dancing She nearly felt totally content to bleed in and out of the mystery that only skies can know, only mountains touch, only stars breathe.

Mary Alice, after that, almost acquired the habit of happiness. For two years her skin sang songs to her bones as she worked, but in any case, she died three years later, tired from too much work, but triumphant.

THE FAT LADY
AND THE SNAKE CHARMER

...for in that sleep of death, what dreams may come?
Shakespeare

I was having my third lunch on Wednesday...have to eat nearly every minute to keep the scales tipped at five hundred...was having my third lunch when Cybele walked by with her Python wrapped all around her. "Get that damned thing away from me when I'm eating," I said for the millionth time since she joined our sideshow.

"He's cold and old. Do you know what it's like to be an old, cold snake? He can't keep warm like we can. He's got no good furnace. The heat's broken in my trailer again. I've got to keep him on me to keep him warm. He's so old; he could go any day now. He's been with me since I was a girl. I'll be sixty next month." She curled her sexy red lips down in a frown, and her long black hair fell over her eyes.

"You sure don't look it," I told her to make her feel good. "You still look thirty." I knew she had a hard life, lots of broken hearts, mean men. Not like me. I always liked good food better than sex.

"I'll never train another like him in my life time. Do you know he's the biggest snake any tamer has lived with, the biggest in captivity, largest trained reptile in the world, nearly!" She sat down across from me and petted his snaked head in her lap... His ever open eyes seemed to look directly into hers as his tongue darted toward her lips. "My king's dying," she moaned. "Do you know how many years it took me to train and tame and show a big guy like him off? You have to get one when it's a baby and play with it every day so it will obey you!"

"Never met one I'd want to obey me!"...can't stand snakes at all."What about those other two big ones you got? They'll do. They're long and impressive enough!"

"Oh, those Boa Constrictors are tiny compared to my king, and too unpredictable to love. I can't stand how I'll miss him! I've got to keep him warm. It's warmer in here. My poor baby. How am I going to live without him?" She was inconsolable. Her dark old eyes clouded as she stroked his long sleek neck.

"I'd rather have a milkshake any day. The pleasure is so delectable. You're skinny as a rail. That's why you keep him wrapped around you. To stay warm; not 'cause he's cold!" I told her like I always did. "You better put some meat on those bones of yours, Cybele! Here. Have some of these good chocolates with me. I ordered them from Paris! How about one of these Italian pastries, all creamy and gooey! They got a great bakery in this town First thing I do when we arrive in a new location is check out the yellow pages for bakeries." She always checks the pet supply shops for fresh rats and rabbits for her king, first thing! "Can't you at least get him to keep his tongue in his mouth while I'm eating?" I told her for the hundredth time. "He makes me sick!"

"Oh, Bertha-Jean, calm down. He won't lick you. That's how he smells and senses the world around him," she told me for the hundredth time. "He knows there's lots of juicy flesh around. Don't worry! He won't lick your snatch!" Cybele laughed and teased me as she always did about hating men and sex.

"All I know is it's a damned forked tongue that thing's got and I don't trust it, so keep it out of my Fettucine Alfredo!"

"Come off it, Bertha-Jean! You know you're afraid of his forking your fat snatch for a cream puff!" She laughed and I laughed, too. I was glad to see her joking again. She was so depressed about her king getting old and dying. I still can't believe she did what she did...just for that big old snake...she always talked about his pretty patterns...how he moved in a sensual dance...how beautiful he was...said she'd rather feel a snake crawl over her than eat a hot fudge sundae any day. Skinny thing...I can't figure her out...knew her for years and couldn't understand what she saw in him.... wonder if that old fat snake tickled her tits with his tongue?...or what?...she was actually once a Bengali Princess...disowned by her father for running away with a lover who deserted her...dark, tall, muscular and slender...her eyes looked right through into your stomach or heart...whichever was more important to you, in my case it's obvious...she said she didn't want to live without him...she was proud, strong, tall, a Cretan Goddess in her costume...she used to dress up like that museum statue you see in art history books...the bare chested lady with the snakes held out in her hands. With the long gold skirt and crown head dress she'd let the snakes crawl over her nakedness while the crowds ogled....but she was getting too old for her act...strange how everyone wants to be something else...the young old; old, young; fat, skinny; skinny fat; black, white; while the whites lie out in the sun trying to get black; kinky haired people straighten theirs, while straight haired ones spend millions to curl theirs...flowers into plastic...pastries like flowers...well...she died just the way she wanted to...the other freaks thought it was disgusting...but I knew it was what she wanted...it's peculiar...unless you knew her as I did...though I can't altogether understand a person who hates food and loves snakes like she did...she just locked herself in with them...she only had those Boas for a year or two...damned snakes take forever to know you...she bought them full grown...said she didn't have time to raise them from babies...said she'd never have as big a Python as her king again... she holed up with him while he was dying and told us all to stay away from her trailer, 'cause he needed quiet...going fast...those Boas got awful hungry...she got awful weak from not eating along with her dying king...some say it was terrible...but I say she got to die like a Cretan Goddess, just the way she wanted...lying there on her satin bed with him all wrapped around her, dead, too...and the others, each one swallowed one of her arms up to the shoulders...she was being slowly ingested and she knew snakes and knew that was what would happen. She looked like a Cretan Goddess when I found her with Boa Constrictors for arms and a satin Python for a dress...she was smiling peacefully...they were part of her...became part reptile...all together...the charmed and the charmer...one...together...chose her own death to be part of her life...how many of us get to?

    ....*In a dark green jungle, beyond the literary cliche of eating ripe oranges an orange is being eaten. Hands curl around its globe; finger-nails dig spongy skin, tearing membrane from segment, as a squirt of juice spurts from a rip made in the sweet flesh. Fingers pull one section from another to make an opening, peeling skin from skin. Fingers more actual than Freudian, press into a moist opening from which juice oozes more freely than from a D.H. Lawrence fig, more freely than from the orange in your mind as you read. A thing once whole is separated from itself; oozes from its being. A mouth like a cave of death takes it in. Teeth mash its juice from it as it swims in its own blood, like a body eaten by a shark, exploded by a bomb, wracked by hunger, tortured by insanity, destroyed by greed, obsessed with lust, digested and become one with its eater, become its eater's flesh and blood.*

More profoundly than fresh oil-stain sinks into unfinished wood, as certainly as dye penetrates cotton, as completely as hydrogen mixes with oxygen to become water, the orange is a part of the living animal, crouched in the darkness, eating, as mind is feeling in the blood and blood is in the mind coursing through the brain of it, there is no pure thought or real abstraction, but chemical formulas of the blood of which we are all a part in the body of the mind, of death which plucks fruit from a tree in a dark green jungle, and the cave of death which is the mouth of mind become the womb of thought full of breath and moist tongue gives birth to the word.

THE CAPITULATION

*And you will join the big brass band
and with your trumpet in your hand,
you'll march in step with all the rest.*

Bertolt Brecht

Trapped within a giant forest enclosure by a high rock wall which stretches farther than I can see beyond the big grassy meadow, I find myself confronted by their hulking bodies, the vacant hurt-beast stare in their eyes. Never before have I felt so small, helpless and weak that it seems the wind with one glancing blow can destroy me.

There's no shelter from them. Just sleek rock cliffs behind me and a large outcropping behind which I've been cowering for so many hours now that I'm no longer sure for what length of time I've knelt in the grass with my hands and chest pressed to the hard rocky surface behind which I'm hiding. I crouch lower behind my sheltering rock and view the situation with constancy. I can feel a fire starting at the base of my neck and shooting off pin-points of flame like firecrackers in my ears. Directly behind me, a small clump of shrubs and trees shields my back from their gaze. By leaning slightly to the right, I can peek out from my hiding place and watch their slow but graceful movements, the lumbering of their great black bodies, their mountainous backs of fur, as they move about making languid trips back and forth to a large pond far ahead to the right of me in a clearing.

I can barely see that a huge rock wall adjoins the far side of the water, so that even if I managed to get to the water and swim out faster than they might follow,

I would come flat up against the high mossy unscalable wall to the far side of the pond. There is no escape but through their midst, though all sorts of schemes skitter through my mind. For a moment, I feel as though I've sprouted wings and will fly over them, a wishful dream. I fairly leap into the air, but a sudden loud snarling sound from one of them brings me to my senses. I look back at the trees behind me. Perhaps, there's some way I can build a ladder, weave a rope, do something before I go mad or reveal myself, but I haven't a single tool other than my bare hands, not even a penknife with me. Only the thick growth of blossoming, berry brambles in front of me and some pines to my right, plus the wayward direction of the wind must be blocking my aroma from their keen noses.

I begin to feel around my feet in the grass for a stone, a stick, anything which I can fashion to give myself the illusion of being less than completely defenseless against their huge hulks, strong legs and fierce claws. My wits are failing me. I think I feel tears sting my eyes, but one doesn't weep when there's no hope at all in view. Even the most daring athlete could not scale the high smooth rock wall behind me. I lament that my curiosity for the woods and its gorgeous wildlife has gotten me into this predicament. I imagine climbing a tree, but remember how superior these beasts are in that endeavor. How long can I last here without food or water before they notice me?

Just as it seems my brain will burst from the strain of studying what is an insolvable and deadly entrapment, they seem to cluster near the edge of the water. The sun is setting as they seem to rumble about in a group. Mothers and cubs seem to rub and sniff each others' snouts in communion as the moon begins to rise higher and brighter and the forest darken with shadows falling over the Rock Oaks and Hemlocks, Maples, Grey Birches and Hickory. Then I see the strangest thing! The big creatures seem to be come from every angle of the forest into the clearing by the pond. One large black beast passes uncomfortably near my hiding place. Their pace seems to quicken with urgency. I watch in fascinated horror as they mull near the edges of the water. There are ten of them them now fishing in the stream. Catching Blue-gilled Sunfish with their long claws and shredding them in their teeth. They fight over a large carp one has managed to claw.

I'm glad that the fish distracts them. I feel my pulse beating against the rock or is it the vibrations of their colossal steps, the earth shaking with their enormous weighty movements. My hands clutch the surface of my sheltering rock so tightly that my fingers turn white. The throbbing in my wrists is one with the pumping of my heart. I feel I will faint and that it will be merciful to do so and not feel the inevitable crushing, tearing blows of their tremendous claws and teeth.

I can't believe what's happening. The surface of the rock seems to slip beneath my grasping palms. Slowly the earth beneath me begins to throb. All the creatures seem to stare in my direction with their hurt-beast eyes. I turn from their gaze and leap up and dash toward the trees with a sense of fear so complete that it's hardly distinguishable from ecstasy, the kind of emotion that turns the whole body liquid and numb. I charge so fast that I nearly smash head-on into the nearest tree which I climb with superhuman strength. I can't recall as I perch on a high branch which footholds or barky protuberances I managed to use to propel me upward, but as my mind returns from its utter hysteria and my consciousness floods back from the thoughtless realm of primitive survival in which it has been suspended, I find myself clinging to a leafy branch. Blood drips from my palms onto the leaves in my grasp and falls in tiny rivulets down my shins onto the brown bark of the branch upon which I crouch in terror, balanced precariously high above the ground, just at the height where the tree begins to spread its leafy branches.

....a salesman far off in the city is having dinner with a client. The client enjoys smoking big cigars and drinking a great deal of gin. The salesman desperately wants his commission and needs it in order to live and keep his job. The salesman smokes a big cigar given him by the client, though he hates the taste of cigars. He drinks gin, though he prefers wine. He's supposed to be on a diet for his heart trouble, but he eats a thick rare steak with the client because the client loves thick rare steak. He is smiling more than his face wants to and his jaws ache. The muscles at the corners of his mouth strain with smiling at everything the client says. He wants to be having dinner with his lover. She is angry that he's always busy entertaining clients and can't manage to dine with her. She's threatened to leave him for his constant neglect. He's supposed to call her and it's getting very late. The client keeps asking stupid, drunken questions. He won't close the deal, but is getting closer and closer to doing so. The salesman has to urinate but is afraid to leave the client alone to think things over or change his mind. The salesman's bladder is going into an excruciating spasm and his mouth burns from the hot cigar, but he goes on smiling and talking agreeably, nodding affirmation to everything the client says....

I'm aware of nothing for a moment but my heavy breathing and a sharp ache in my chest. Then the big beasts begin to sway in rhythm towards where I perch hiding. Their big furry bodies rock to and fro as they come swaying toward me *en masse*—raising first a front leg and then a hind leg, one after the other: One two, one two, one two, in swaying repetition all of them begin to dance and shake the earth and the tree in which I quake.

Surely it will be uprooted by the force of their giant paws and plummet me to the ground. They dance under me as though they are surely plotting my destruction beneath their great black skulls. One shakes the tree with his giant paws as another climbs upward onto his back. Then I feel its wet nose against my ankle and I slip and slide down its warm back and down the back of the one beneath it and onto the ground into the midst of their staring eyes.

I see bright red color pound in my eyes. I, too, am dancing, dancing with the Black Bears of the mountains of Sussex County, stomping the earth in rhythm with their big feet, as much as a person can dance the dance of the wild bear, and as long as I dance with them they do not trample or claw me, as long as I dance and keep on dancing the dance of the wild bears of this Delaware Valley, dancing their dance, they do not, they will not destroy me.

THE PSYCHIC TOUCH

Hearts are not had as a gift, but hearts are earned
By those who are not entirely beautiful;
Yet many that have played the fool
For beauty's very self has charm made wise,
And many a poor man that has roved,
Loved and thought himself beloved,
From a glad kindness cannot take his eyes.

W. B. Yeats

He stretched and lifted his hands into the tiger-striped sunlight glancing through the venetian blinds. His fifteen fingers fluttered amid dancing moats. He blinked his eyes and sat up. The room was hot. The Indian Summer sun fell in streaks across the bed. It was the first morning of his life, since he was a child, that he had not wakened to the sounds and smells of a circus: elephants being watered; caged animals growling for their breakfasts; the smell of straw and damp canvas; Donald the Dwarf singing "O What a Beautiful Morning..." and Cream Puff, the fat lady, telling Donald the Dwarf to shut up, that it was never a beautiful morning until after she'd had her first breakfast; chains rattled; stakes hammered; the aroma of strong coffee from the chow wagon. It was the first morning he had ever awakened leisurely, in a hotel room, to nothing but the whirring of distant traffic far below his windows.

He had made up his mind to try living in the world of normal people. At last he had the courage to try it. He had quietly handed in his resignation, collected his pay check and small savings, and slipped away just as the circus was closing down for the night, before anyone could question him or say "Goodbye," he was gone as the lights went out in the big tent and the tentflaps of the side shows were tied shut for the night.

He hoped he would never hear the voice of a Circus Barker again:

"Step right this way, Ladies and Gentlemen. See the Phenomenal Man with Three Arms! You haven't seen anything until you've seen The Man with Three Arms. He'll daze you, he'll dazzle and amaze you. See him juggle a dozen eggs at one time, play piano and flute all at once. See him perform amazing feats of super-human dexterity, using all three arms and fifteen fingers to daze you, to entertain and amaze you. Right this way, Ladies and Gentleman, to the Phenomenal Man with Three Arms."

It was 11:30 A.M. He'd made it all the way through breakfast in the hotel coffee shop without anyone noticing. He had kept his second right arm quietly at his side. He had kept it from fluttering with excitement as it always did when he'd tried to hide it under his jacket before, kept it from suddenly popping open the buttons of his jacket and flying out to aid him in the buttering of toast, or scratching his ear as his other hands were busily involved in the task of holding fork or knife while lifting coffee cup to lips. Anyone looking at him through breakfast would have thought that he was an ordinary human being; perhaps a little fatter on his right side beneath his jacket where his third arm added a slight bulge to the right side of his torso, but an ordinary enough fellow, quietly breakfasting in the coffee shop of a hotel, perhaps on a business trip away from his wife and family, maybe an ordinary salesman or a lawyer or a department store buyer. No one would ever have guessed, he told himself proudly, with what strain and careful control, with what perturbation and anxiety, he kept his third arm pressed to his side so as not to reveal his identity.

He wiped his chin, folded his napkin, and stood up just as a pretty woman he had been watching, seated in a booth across from him, stood to leave. He carefully picked up his check with one hand while he reached for his wallet with another hand, all the while straining to keep his third firmly at his side. He followed her through the aisle of tables, watching her buttocks move under her white mini-skirt, noticing how the smooth backs of her knees and calves fitted her creaseless flesh-colored stockings.

They were standing at the cashier's counter side by side. He breathed the delicate perfume she wore. He watched her slender fingers open her purse and pull out three one dollar bills from the zippered compartment in the lining. She looked sideways at him and smiled. She must have been aware that he was watching her. After all, he was a pleasant looking fellow as long as he kept his secret. He might even be taken for quite a handsome man. He watched her close her purse, snapping it shut, and he saw her hand lose its grasp on the handle. It seemed to happen in slow motion. He grabbed for it just before it hit the floor. It was too late. She saw it all: his jacket fly open, his third arm reach out automatically as it did, his other hands still involved with holding his breakfast check and wallet. It was too late. It had happened as it always did. With grace and dexterity, his third hand retrieved the falling pocket book and revealed what he had so painstakenly managed to keep hidden.

She gasped, almost screamed a little. He placed the purse on the counter and fled through the revolving doors as fast as he could, his face burning. There was no use to explain. There was never any use explaining. He could feel the young woman and the cashier staring after him in amazement and fear. He could hear the polite, "Thank you," that had frozen on the young woman's lips when she was startled by the fact that it was a *third* hand on the end of a *third* arm pushing up from under his jacket that held her purse out to her.

It was 2:00 P.M. He was back in his hotel room stretched out on the bed, lying on his back, two hands cradling his head, the third hand holding a burning cigarette. He watched the smoke curl toward the ceiling. It seemed to float up from the pain in his stomach, the dull ache in his chest, the burning sensation in his eyes. The smoke became the scream he couldn't scream, the silent sound of his own agony, floating up and widening, thinning out and dispersing.

He had rushed from the coffee shop and walked blindly through the park at the center of town. He had wanted to keep on trying. He had bought a newspaper and sat down on 1 bench to read, his third arm concealed beneath his jacket. A young mother and her small boy joined him on the bench. The child ran off to play ball. The mother asked to borrow the entertainment section of the newspaper. He complied. She began to chat, as a stranger chats out of politeness, about the headlines, when suddenly the little boy tossed his ball out of control in the wrong direction. As it hurled toward him, up flew his third arm, reflexively, to catch the stray ball before it smashed into the newspaper which he held open, with his other two hands, before him. Suddenly there it was: intercepting the ball and shocking the young mother into amazement, fascinating the wide-eyed child. He jumped up and ran leaving the newspaper and ball on the bench behind him. He had run as before, too exasperated, too defeated, to want to explain.

For four hours, cigarette smoke had been rising to the ceiling from his defeat. Already he knew the position of every crack and paint chip in the ceiling over his bed and he had wanted to know the life outside in the city.

He put out his last cigarette and crumpled the empty pack. It landed with a metallic thud in the waste can, where a flick of his third wrist gracefully tossed it. He thought of the dexterity of his three hands, the hours, the lifetime of practice that had gone into training his third arm to respond automatically in juggling, in playing the piano, in performing all the tasks of everyday living. He thought of all the things which he could do that normal people couldn't do. He could tie two pairs of shoelaces at once. He could unlock the door while holding several bundles of parcels. He could comb and smooth the hair on both sides of his head at one time. He could shave both sides of his face at once and dress himself, tie his tie and zipper his fly, in half the time it took an ordinary man. He could write things down and shuffle through papers while holding the telephone to his ear with his third hand; he could hold the telephone book open and keep his finger on the number he wanted to call while depositing a dime and holding the receiver all at once; he could open a can, working the opener with two hands, and holding the can still with a third; he could play piano and one-handed flute simultaneously. He could bake and cook while holding a bowl, whipping its contents, reading the cook book, and adding ingredients all at once. He could smoke and light a cigarette, and hold a book he was reading without interruption or loss of place. In the shower, he could hold the soap and washcloth and scrub his back and stomach all at once. He could pat his head, rub his stomach, and scratch his nose besides. To be perfectly truthful, he was *superior* to a normal man.

He was more capable of work, of lifting, of painting, of typing, of musicianship, of almost any skill one could think of, and yet, the irony of his deformity was that he was made to feel inferior, a freak, a misfit, with no place but the circus to hide. Not one of his feats of skill and dexterity was worth the pain of alienation he felt from the rest of humanity. He would have given up all his skill for the love of one woman, for the chance to have a normal life out in the world of normal men.

He had many erotic dreams of how well he could make love to a woman with all three of his arms and hands working at once to stimulate and arouse her to desire for him, but always, the pleasant dreams were interrupted by a look of revulsion on the woman's face as he undressed and revealed his third arm.

It was not that he was innocent. He had managed to have some sexual experience around the circus. He had been to bed with a bareback rider who really preferred horses to men, but she made him promise only to touch her with two hands, and she had wanted the lights out so that the room was pitch black. He had made love with the snake charmer. She had enjoyed his hands roaming all over her body. She said he reminded her of the snakes she loved better than men. He had even been to bed with Cream Puff, the fat lady, but she had felt like her name, and *she*, he was ashamed to admit to himself, had repulsed *him*. He had copulated with a dwarf woman and sodomized a queer clown, but he had never been near, or touched a single woman, or man, whom he had truly wanted and admired, let alone loved.

He would have given any and all of his superior skill and dexterity to be normal, to be free to find the love of a normal woman. The thought of doing so made his groin ache, as he lay on his bed. He turned over and burying his face in his hands, grabbed his crotch with his third, curled his knees up to his chest and wept softly, until he slept quietly, and light left the windows as shadows collected in corners of the room, and the furniture listened to his breathing with still and wooden empathy.

The girls's body was discovered by her mother who became suspicious when her daughter did not answer the telephone for several days running. The assailant inflicted several wounds about the head and chest with a pen-knife found in the stairwell of the apartment building where the girl lived. Police believe her to be the fifth victim of the assailant who has been terrorizing the city for the past three months. Police are continuing an investigation into the deaths of....

She shivered and clicked off the radio. She was tired. She ran a comb through her short blond hair, pulled her skirt down over her plump hips and stepped into her shoes. She tucked a novel, *The End of the Road*, by John Barth, into her handbag, fitted the strap over her shoulder, locked the apartment door securely being careful to leave the hall and bedroom lights burning, pressed the button, and waited for the elevator.

"Another night of hustling drinks," she thought, but, she told herself, as she always did: "It's better than hustling my body." She wished she could completely obliterate her life of two years ago from her memory—not out of an indignant sense of morality or injured pride, not even out of guilt so much as out of sorrow for time wasted, time spent in quiet submission, time lived in being dead, giving herself over and over again to someone else's sensation until she wanted to crawl out of her flesh.

The subway screeched and rattled and swayed,

carrying its cargo of human paranoia through the dark tunnel. She found herself looking at the blackheads on the large nose of the man hanging from a strap beside her He smiled and she looked down and away. "Men, with their stubborn angry persistent bodies. Their indifference. Their way of holding and grabbing you to feel for themselves, never thinking of making you feel your own body," she thought. "Just wanting for themselves."

She lifted the counter top entrance to the circular bar and clicked it shut behind her. There he was sitting on the same stool he had been sitting on for two weeks. She liked his face. She felt a kinship with that certain look of sadness that seemed to flood the screen behind his eyes. She liked his hands: the way he held his drink. Counting the change in the register, she reflected for a moment on how she was attracted to a man by his hands. If she could look closely at a man's hands and imagine them touching her breasts, then she could imagine enjoying his making love to her.

"You're two dollars short, Harry," she chidded the bartender who worked the afternoon shift. Harry stood behind her at the register. "That's three fifty you owe me this week altogether."

She went around to the other side of the bar where the man who'd been there all week sat on his stool. "Are you all set?" she asked, smiling.

"No," he said, "I'll take another bourbon on the rocks just to celebrate your arrival on this momentous occasion." he gestured broadly.

They had talked a bit and she had learned of his work as booking and publicity agent for the circus. "What momentous occasion?" she queried, still smiling.

"I did a good job today. Completed the last of my bookings for eight months ahead. Every space on that endless chart is full for eight long months in advance. Now it will be no sweat. Just paperwork, advance publicity and mailing contracts." Actually, he was thinking about the momentous occasion of having gotten through fourteen days of walking around the city, shopping in stores and eating in restaurants without his secret arm detected.

"Congratulations!" She handed him his drink. "This one's on the house. You deserve it." She smiled warmly as he lifted the glass to his lips. She wondered why he had nowhere more interesting than the bar she worked in to spend his evenings.

"Thanks, won't you join me, or is it too early in the evening?" he teased.

"It's too early," She indicated the after-office-hours crowd that had begun to file in. "Maybe later."

It had been a very busy Friday night. "Will that be all, sir? Or, will you have another? I'm surprised that stool you're sitting on hasn't buckled its knees for a rest," she chortled.

There were minnows swimming in his stomach. His head burned and felt liquid as though it would simply run down like hot wax over his shoulders. "One more double bourbon," he heard himself say, and his voice sounded unfamiliar as though he were talking underwater.

She set the drink in front of him. Her hand seemed to move in slow motion: the pale fingers with gleaming nails slid the glimmering bronze liquid toward him.

He'd taken to making short trips out during the day. Spending a few hours wandering in the city, through parks and museums, with his third arm hidden, was far easier on his nervous system. For two weeks now, he had spent evenings in the hotel bar, watching her as she served drinks and chatted amiably with the customers. It was easy to sit there observing her and pretending to watch the television screen just above the bar mirror. The act of simply lifting a drink to his lips was simple to execute in a relaxed manner with his third arm quiet and secret beneath his jacket. It didn't require any great amount of concentration. It was so much easier than eating an entire meal in public: his third arm straining at his side as he held it back from aiding in the more complicated procedures of cutting meat, stirring sugar into coffee, buttering bread. Two whole weeks had passed without a single unwanted move of that arm.

Every move she made had become predictable to him. He found himself vaguely calculating that he must have spent something like sixty hours just watching her. This was the first night he had allowed himself to become quite so full of liquor. He told himself that it was time to leave, to go back to his silent room, to lie in the dark thinking of her, touching himself and dreaming of touching her, making love to her, until his thighs trembled and he released a small groan into the silence, and a feeling of self-hatred or hurt pride or sheer dull loneliness pulled him into sleep.

Instead, he hung on, sipping slowly one more drink of the several he had lost count of, until he realized that the National Anthem was playing and the flag waving on the T.V. screen, signing off the channel for the night. He looked at the clock to the left of the bar. 2:00 A.M. She was counting up the night's receipts, rattling cash in the register. He had pondered before, as he did now, why such a bright and seemingly lovely creature was working as a barmaid in a hotel. The place was respectable enough, not a dive like some he had seen in his walks around the city. He couldn't figure it out. Once he had asked her what she was doing tending bar and she'd replied: "Nothing! just making a living and trying to figure out what I should be doing. Besides," she added, "there are a lot worse ways of making a buck, and I enjoy talking with people, like you. It's interesting, and jobs aren't that easy to come by lately in this city."

He had felt a significance in her tone when she said that there were a lot worse ways of making a living. He wondered if she'd ever been a prostitute, if that was what she'd meant to imply. She smiled cheerfully whenever she answered a question put to her by any of the customers. She smiled cheerfully at him, too. He thought that her face was prettier when she wasn't smiling. It had a certain sad silent repose that was very appealing to him; made him wonder what was behind the sorrow in the eyes. He had tried to remember her face when he lay alone in bed, dreaming of making love to her.

He looked around the bar and realized that he was the only man left sitting there. One other fellow was putting on his hat and coat near the coat rack. When he finished he exited, leaving silence behind him.

"Well," she said. "I'll have to close up now."

"Oh, yes, of course. Guess I'm a little under the weather. I didn't realize how late it was," he answered apologetically.

"Oh, that's all right. I was busy counting up the receipts anyway. Are you going to finish this one?"

He took the glass from her hand and downed the last few gulps of bourbon. "Thanks," he said and left five dollars on the bar.

"Thank you." She slipped the bills into her skirt pocket.

"Do you live far from here?" he found himself

asking in a strangely calm voice.

"Not very," she answered casually.

"I just thought I'd see you home, if you like, since I'm here so late. I could use a little walk and you might like some company."

"I was going to take a cab, but if you really feel like walking a little, it would be nice if you'd walk me. It's only seven blocks."

"I'd be glad to," he answered.

"Great, the boss will be here to lock up the receipts and close up any minute."

"It must be exciting working for the circus. I never met anyone who worked for the circus before."
" "It's all right sometimes, but, I can think of other things I'd like to do." They had already gone a block. He was steady on his feet though he felt they might without notice give way under him. Strangely, he felt so much more in control of his arm—as if it were the drunkest part of him and had fallen dead asleep under his jacket. He felt unusually calm. He took her by the elbow as they crossed the street. She didn't react, or try to draw her arm away. They had made a lot of small talk in the bar, but never concerning anything personal.

"Will you be in town much longer?"

"A few more weeks while I finish up arranging advance publicity."

"Are you married?"

"No, I'm not." He was elated that she was interested enough to ask. "Why? Are you?"

"Oh, I was just curious. I guess it would be difficult to be married and do your kind of work, traveling around all the time."

"Are you?" he repeated.

"No, I'm not married, and I don't want to be!"

"Why not? A pretty girl like you must have a hard time keeping single."

"Thanks, but it's easier than you can imagine. The only men who have asked are men I couldn't stand, so it's been easy. Besides, from what I've seen of marriage, I think I can do without it!"

He liked the way she talked without putting on airs. She seemed to say whatever she was thinking without calculating the effect. There was an uncomfortable silence. His third arm twitched under his jacket. He cleared his throat. They would be at her door in a few more steps and he didn't know how to approach her. "I guess I had a few more drinks than usual tonight. It gets pretty lonely when you have to be in a strange town all the time. You get tired of calling up people you hardly know or haven't seen in a long time just to have someone to talk to. I like talking to you. Can I buy you some coffee? Maybe you'd like a little breakfast?"

"I'm awful tired. But maybe, well, if you wouldn't take it wrong, you could come upstairs for some coffee. Just for a little while. My feet hurt. They always hurt at night when I'm done. I'd like to get out of these shoes."

"Ouch! Hot!" He scalded his tongue on the coffee.

"Oh, I'm sorry; it is awful hot," she said, standing in the doorway of the tiny kitchen. Her apartment was neat and very carefully arranged. There was nothing expensive in it, but it was very comfortable with homey touches everywhere. It was completely furnished in varying shades of blue. Light blue curtains, dark blue rug, bright blue couch and electric blue pillows. Blue vases. Blue tablecloth. Even blue paper napkins with blue porcelain cups. He liked the idea of everything being blue.

"It's very peaceful in here," he said. "All the blue makes it very peaceful."

"I like it that way. The monochromatic effect is the way I like it. The bedroom is all in shades of green. I'll show you on your way out. It's near the door." She talked about how she had always wanted to be a writer, but hadn't been able to finish school. Her parents had died in a car crash after she had been at the city university for only a year. She supposed they had crashed while arguing fiercely, as they always had. She'd been working ever since.

It was so exciting to be in her home, to see how she lived.

"What kind of work have you done?" he asked, trying to hide his intense curiosity.

"I've been...well, to tell you the truth, I'd rather not talk about it. It would be easy to lie, but I've decided not to do that anymore. I just don't tell people about it until I've known them longer."

He wondered what she meant by that. He thought now that she probably had been a hustler or a prostitute. He wanted to tell her that it didn't matter, that he understood her sadness, that he understood the feeling of having to sell yourself, but he didn't dare.

"Do you smoke?" she asked.

"Sorry," he lied, "I don't have any cigarettes with me." He couldn't risk smoking in front of her—not when everything was going so well—because it was something he usually did with his third arm, nonchalantly, while his others performed more necessary tasks.

"No, no, I mean grass. Do you smoke grass? I've got some good stuff. Not the best, but it will do!" She went over to a cabinet and pulled out a little blue plastic box and opened it. She rolled herself a joint and lit it. She took a long drag on it, held her breath, and offered it to him. He watched her in silence, pretending to listen to the music she had put on the player: some female folk singer. He watched her carefully, pretending to look at her hands as she rolled the joint, but he was watching her breasts: the way the button-hole on her blue blouse was stretched wider where her breasts bulged under the cloth. He imagined his mouth on hers as his fingers undid the button. Ever so gently, he imagined sliding his hand beneath the cloth.

"It's pretty good grass," she said. "Have some!"

"No thanks," he answered, "not with all this juice in me. I don't like to mix them."

"Well, would you like more coffee? I'd like to keep talking but I'm getting awfully sleepy. Thanks so much for walking me home. I can always use the cab fare for something more important. It's scary walking home alone around here at two in the morning."

"It was my pleasure. Maybe I'll see you at the bar tomorrow evening."

"Oh, no, I'll be going on vacation for a whole week starting today and boy, do I need it. A whole week's vacation. I saved it up from the summer so that I could just spend a whole week relaxing at home. I always get such a lazy feeling and feel so sad at this time of year that I can't bear to work so I save up my summer vacation and take it during early October." She sighed. "'These are the days when birds come back, a very few, a bird or two to take a backward look. These are the days when skies resume the old old sophistries of June, a blue and gold mistake...' That's a poem by

Emily Dickinson. I was studying American poetry just before I had to quit school." She looked at the ceiling.

"It's nice," he said, thinking about how he'd never read any poetry.

"Anyway, I'd rather work in summer because the bar's air-conditioned and it gets hotter than hell in this place in summer."

"Maybe you could get yourself a little air-conditioner cheap now. Wouldn't they be on sale this time of year?"

"An air-conditioner. I wouldn't own such a thing. Don't you realize what an ecological disaster air-conditioning is? A guy who came in the bar just last week was telling me about it. He works for a scientific magazine and he's writing an article on how air-conditioning makes a city like this hotter. You have to burn up a lot of energy to run all those air-conditioners and they pour a lot of hot air into the streets. Air-conditioning makes the whole damn city hotter as a result. It's a diminishing return. Counter-productive. It's ridiculous! I wouldn't own one of those things if you gave it to me. I don't eat beef either, because a steer consumes more protein from the land than it gives back. It's wasteful and decadent to eat meat when so many people are starving...Wow, this grass is really getting to me. I'll see you in a week if you're still in town! Thanks again for walking me home."

"Thanks for the coffee," he said, trying to think of a way to ask her to go out with him, but he didn't dare ask her to go to dinner. It would be too difficult to control his arm at an entire dinner. "Maybe you'd like to go to a movie tomorrow night..." He started to gain the courage to ask her as he stood up, but he stood too quickly: the table jiggled and the cup fell forward on its saucer. He grabbed for it, thinking of the blue tablecloth, but it was too sudden a move. His third arm flew out from under his jacket, grabbing the cup just before it overturned.

She was staring at him. Her expression showed surprise and then terror. "What, what was that?" she gasped. "Was that...did I see... am I seeing another..."

"Yes," he said, "you are seeing another arm. It's only an arm. I have three arms. It's really not so terrible. You don't have to look so frightened!"

"I can't help it, I'm sorry, but I don't know what to say...I feel kind of high, like I'm not seeing right. I never heard of...I mean I've never seen...I..."

"I lied to you. I'm not a publicity or booking agent for the circus! I'm a performer, one of the side show attractions, The Phenomenal Man with Three Arms. I perform all sorts of tricks and things. I could show you. Maybe, I could come back tomorrow and show you some of the things I can do." But it was too late; he saw the look of surprise and fear and dread and knew she was trying to think of a way to get rid of him. He found himself moving toward her and talking rapidly, saying all the things he had rehearsed for two weeks in the dark of his room since he had first seen her. He could not bear having failed again. He would make her understand: "I can do all kinds of things. Do you have some eggs I could juggle? You don't have a piano or a flute. I could show you how I tie two shoelaces at once..." His arms were around her. His mouth groped for hers. She stiffened, pulled back in horror, and screamed. His third hand went over her mouth and muffled her screams. She struggled.

"Don't scream," he said, "and I'll let you talk!" He took his hand away from her mouth.

"I can't...I can't...I'm scared. Please don't hurt me..." The words tumbled out of her mouth in a confused jumble.

"Hurt you? I don't want to hurt you; I want to love you, but, don't scream. I just want to love you. Stop looking at me that way! I'm so tired." He heard his voice come out in sobs.

She pulled away and ran toward the door. He was quicker. He grabbed her around the waist with two arms and held her shoulder with another. She screamed. He covered her mouth with his third hand and, holding her tightly, he pulled her to the floor. He was half lying on top of her.

"Don't be frightened; I won't hurt you. I like you; I want to make love to you," he said, controlling his voice. "Just don't scream and I won't hurt you!" Slowly, he took his hand away from her mouth. She stared into his face; then she struggled; she wouldn't stay still.

"Let me go; please let me go," she pleaded quietly.

"No, I can't let you go," he answered firmly.

She pushed her knee into his groin and struggled and then she screamed again. He slapped her face. He had never used his third hand to slap anyone; in fact, he'd never hit anyone at all, but he slapped her hard.

"Don't scream! Just don't scream. Please, I don't want to hurt you! I don't want to hurt you," he repeated, sobbing.

With his third hand, he was unbuttoning her blouse. He tore it open and tore at the white cotton brassiere, exposing her right breast. His other two hands kept her shoulders pinned tightly to the floor as he lay heavily upon her. She couldn't breathe; everything went dark; she gasped and felt as if she were being crushed to death by any octopus; an octopus was sucking at her breast.

He felt her go limp beneath him. He was

frightened. If only she hadn't looked at him that way!

He lifted her dead weight in his arms and placed his ear to her chest. Her heart was beating. He carried her into the bedroom and put her on the bed. Turning on the light, he noticed her breasts rising and falling with constricted movement, as if she were having difficulty breathing and might stop any second. Carefully and gently he opened her clothing, her blouse and skirt which seemed to confine her breath. He removed them with his three hands deftly working in unison. Then he sat beside her, watching her begin to breathe more smoothly. Her body seemed the most beautiful sight he'd ever witnessed in his life, more wondrous than flowers, trees, mountains, or meadows. More magnificent than any of the wild beasts, the glorious lions, tigers, horses, elephants or snakes who performed in the circus—a sight so awesome that it struck his contemplating mind with sheer reverence. He couldn't hold himself back any longer. He began to gently stroke her smooth skin, caressing her belly, breasts, hips, thighs with a velvet touch. He pressed his face against her Venus mound, nestling his lips in her pubes. He felt the excitement in his groin rise as he did so. She began to stir and opened her eyes. She seemed about to scream again, but before she could he spoke with soothing assurance.

"Please, don't scream. I won't hurt you. You're so lovely to me. I want to worship your body, to love you, to know what you think and feel. I promise I won't hurt you. I promise. Please understand. I have all the normal feelings of a normal man."

The sound of his voice reminded her of where she was, who she was, and all that had transpired before she'd passed out. She obeyed his words. This time she was afraid not to and realized that it was too late to stop him. She was there on the bed, naked, she realized, and his three hands were touching her and holding her down. She wondered why he was touching her so gently instead of forcing himself roughly into her. His eyes were glazed and she was sure he was manical and not to be reasoned with. She'd had plenty of experience with men.

Reading her mind, he flicked out the light over the headboard. He had read in a book somewhere that women usally prefer sexual contact with new lovers in darkened rooms. He wanted her to relax and feel good, stop being frightened and enjoy his love making. He didn't want to force her.

A faint light streamed in from the living room where a record needle scratched round and round, caught in a final groove. Subconsciously, she saw herself, for an instant, as the heroine of a rape scene in a book she'd read, but fear quickly clouded the image and made what was happening more real than anything she'd ever read. She lay rigidly beneath his hands, fearing to make the slightest move that might provoke him, as his three hands roamed her body, softly pawing and kneading her flesh.

Because of his excessively strong hands, she knew there was little she could do to escape him. If he wanted to murder her, what defense could she offer a man so thoroughly endowed with strength, agility and extra dexterity? Somehow, she did not believe that he was truly violent. His three hands touched her with such awe and gentle persuasion that she was more puzzled than afraid. His hands spoke to every inch of her body from her neck to her toes, and then, he ran his hands over her face and smoothed her forehead and temples as he pressed his lips with an eager passion to hers. He kissed every inch of her face. His breath smelled of bourbon.

For what must have been at least an hour, she lay still, too frightened to move, as he patiently massaged and caressed and kissed her everywhere. She kept wondering why he didn't attack her and satisfy himself. Her life as a prostitute had conditioned her to expect men to want only their own satisfaction and not to think of hers. Yet, every time she made the slightest suggestion of rising from the bed, he would whisper: "Don't get up. Relax. Stay with me!" with such a desperation that she was scared into submission. Very slowly, she began to realize that he was really trying to please and excite her. Still, she couldn't relax for fear of what he might do next: hurt her in some way or strangle her or smother her. The strange feeling of his three hands roaming over her caused fingery patterns of light to flash in her mind. She thought that any minute an involutary scream would burst from her lips, but his patient fingers began to send currents, chemical vibrations, through her body. Somehow, she began, through a kind of human electricity, to know and believe that he wouldn't hurt her.

He made her roll over onto her belly so that he could message her buttocks and back, gently kneading every vertebrae in her spine until she couldn't lie rigidly any longer. Her body began to relax despite her mind.

"I learned this from a circus trapeze artist—the best kind of message in the world. See, I'm not going to hurt you. I wish I could make you want me as I want you. That's all. I just want to make love to you—real love to you—so that you feel so good. Please let me," he spoke as he caressed the backs of her knees and thighs and kneaded her back with his third hand. Then he asked her to roll over again. It seemed two hours had passed as she lay there not speaking while abstract images of tongues and mouths and fingers patterned her brain with soft flesh and rhythms of his hands and musical kisses filled her ears with sounds of skin.

She felt drugged into relaxation. A frightened part of her mind hovered in a corner of the room somewhere like a caught and caged animal, cowering at the scene, but apart from it.

"You're beautiful, " he said softly. "You know now that I won't hurt you. I can feel that you are beginning to trust me. I can feel it in my hands. You can tell that my hands love you. They can't lie. My hands are telling the truth. I only want you to feel good and to want me."

She thought how strange he was: this peculiar man with too many arms and hands, trying relentlessly and patiently to make her feel good and working more earnestly at it than any man she'd ever known.

"Just relax and everything will be all right." He spoke softly again, and she remembered with irony how many times she herself had offered such words to a nervous or young and inexperienced john.

"I want to make you feel better than you've ever felt before," he whispered softly into her ear as his hands glided over her breasts and the fingers of his third hand rubbed her moistened clitoris in gentle constant rhythm. She clenched her teeth. She hadn't allowed anyone to touch her there for so long. She'd learned to dread the acute sensation, the unbearable thrills that always led to disappointment and disillusionment, the excitement that never found an outlet, the pressure cooker that boiled its contents slowly away without exploding. If such a thing as a female orgasm existed, and she was unsure that it did, she'd become resigned to the fact that she wasn't capable of it. She'd learned to avoid her own excitement, to coldly and detachedly submit. She knew how to thrash about and groan a little to fake an orgasm in order to satisfy a john who wanted a response. Acting was easy. If you pretended hard enough that you were satisfied, you almost fooled yourself into thinking you were.

His persistent voice and hands became hypnotic. She felt her nerves erecting beneath his firm but gentle and relentlessly patient touch. She gasped a little as he spread her legs open while his fingers and hands slid in and out and over her. She'd never known anything like the feeling that came over her. Her teeth seemed to tingle in her gums and her stomach muscles twitched as her thighs seemed to turn to liquid. Her torso jerked involuntarily and half rose from the bed. She closed her eyes and sighed and shivered. She was no longer afraid of him. The late hour, the marijuana she'd smoked, her emotional exhaustion, numbed her brain and made her body acutely aware of sensation. She'd never felt such pleasant sensitivity before. She stopped caring about who he was or whether she should trust him. She simply trusted him. A memory of walking to school with her little girl's hand held firmly in her father's large masculine hand surfaced momentarily in her mind and merged with a picture of her father ascending the front steps of her childhood home with a new bicycle for her birthday. Its red metal frame shone brightly in the afternoon sunlight. Her father's smiling face looked into hers with expectation in his eyes. A moan of pleasure escaped her lips.

The man with three arms had removed his clothes and donned a condom. While speaking softly and touching her breasts, he pushed himself slowly into her, filling her and moving in steadily increasing rhythm. All the while telling her: "You're so beautiful. I love you and want you to feel so good. I'm so glad that you want me to make love to you now. I can hear your body talking to my hands now. I can feel you trusting me and wanting me. You feel so beautiful, just as I dreamed you'd be. Just as I've wanted you to be. There's nothing to worry about. I'll be careful. I won't make you pregnant. I've taken care of everything. You can relax and not be worried. You're protected."

His three hands were gently moving over her body, petting her, caressing her breasts and shoulders and face and smoothing her hair and hips. He moved in her for a long time until he seemed to heave in her and expand and she felt heat and throbbing inside and heard him release a huge magnificent groan and moan and sigh. He lay still on her and seemed to sob with relief. Her body ached under his, but she didn't move whether from fear or compassion. Then his three arms held her tightly and he kissed her face and breasts very reverently. She thought it was over, that he would let her up now, but he smothered his face in her breasts and continued to kiss her and held her while his third hand massaged her, gently but firmly back and forth over her delicate nerves. His hands worked ceaselessly. It seemed another hour passed as he patiently attended her body, breathing deeply as if in ecstasy, whispering to her: "Come to me; please come to me!" He kept talking to her and moving his hands and fingers over her. "You're beautiful. I want so much for you to come to me. Please come to me. I want you to feel so good."

His voice and hands were even more hypnotic than before and she began to sigh and breathe deeply and she heard herself speak in a hoarse whisper: "Yes, yes, don't stop; don't stop; it feels so good."

"Oh, yes, my beautiful one, I won't stop. Yes, it feels so good. Yes," he replied with ardency.

Then she groaned all out of herself. Her groin turned to warm liquid waves washing over her and spraying light through her mind, releasing angry demons from her pores, her body jerking with ecstasy as her throat set free an animal scream, an ancient primal cry which he kissed and smothered back into her mouth as he wept with joy, and she submitted herself to him completely, her chest melting into his, her arms around his neck as they sighed and his tears fell on her eyes.

She opened her eyes and found herself lying in her own bed with the sheet pulled up to her neck. She looked around the room in a daze. Her skirt heaped in a ball, with a pair of scissors across it, lay on the edge of the dresser. Her blouse lay on the floor beneath it. Her body ached. She moved a little and her breasts ached under the changing weight of the sheet and blanket. The memory of what had happened the night before came flooding back with the smell of coffee permeating the room. Then she heard clattering noises from the kitchen and realized that she smelled brewing coffee.

She pulled herself up from the bed, feeling her thighs ache and a slight burning sensation between her legs. It occured to her that she should be frightened, but she wasn't. She grabbed her robe from a hook on the inside of the closet door, donned it and wrapped it around her. She looked into the mirror. Her cheeks and lips were red. Her mascara made black smudges under her eyes. She wet her finger and rubbed the smudges away. Then she heard a faint humming and his voice from out in the kitchen sang: "Oh, what a beautiful morning, oh, what a beautiful day. I've got a wonderful feeling. Everything's goin' my way." She heard the sound of a metal pan clanked onto the burner, footsteps on the kitchen linoleum.

She crept out into the hall, running her hand

through her tousled hair. Now, she did feel a chill of fear, or was it a thrill of expectation, or was she a bit dizzy? She swayed and leaned against the cool plaster of the hallway.

There he stood in the kitchen before the stove. He had her blue apron over his shirt and trousers. He turned and smiled at her.

"Good morning," he said. "I'm making you some breakfast. How do you like your eggs: scrambled, sunny-side up, fried, or once over lightly?"

She stared at him blankly and didn't answer. He looked back at her. He looked directly into her eyes and smiled warmly.

"Scrambled," she finally heard herself say. Her voice was soft and husky. She cleared her throat.

With his third arm, he reached for the blue bowl of eggs on the table as, with his other two hands, he put a lump of butter into the frying pan. Then, deftly and more quickly than she had ever seen it done, he cracked the eggs into the pan, deposited their broken shells into the garbage, and scrambled them. His three hands seemed to fly before him with great speed and dexterity.

"Sit down," he said softly. "You must be a little nervous and frightened. Please don't be. You were beautiful last night. You told me that no one had ever made you feel that way, just before you fell asleep. That means a great deal to me. I hope I didn't hurt you. How do you feel?"

Blankly, she looked at him again. He smiled back at her as before. Finally, she sat at the tiny kitchen table. She felt the cold formica on her forearms and elbows. "I feel all right," she said. Her voice shook but was less husky. Now she realized that his shirt had three sleeves sewn into it: two on the right, one just under and a little to the front of the other. He disappeared for a moment into the other room and returned with his jacket on. His third arm was hidden from view.

"I must make you feel nervous," he said. "I'm sorry." He came up behind her and she stiffened.

"Please, please," he said, "don't be afraid." He pressed two hands to her forehead and rubbed her temples and then he messaged her neck and shoulders very gently.

"Coffee's ready," he said. He poured a cup and placed it before her. She didn't respond. He summoned all his courage. "Milk and sugar?" he asked.

"Yes," she answered, and after a long pause: "Thank you."

He felt relieved. He sighed. "Well, what are you going to do today?" he asked cheerfully. "I saw a can of blue enamel and new paint brushes on the hall table. What are they for?"

She looked up at him, wondering at his cheerfulness and nonchalance. "I was going to paint the ceiling in the bathroom again."

"Again?" he asked wryly.

"It's chipping and peeling from the dampness over the shower," she explained.

"Let me do it for you; I can do it in half the time!" he said and laughed.

She knew what he meant. "Okay," she said, and at last, she smiled back at him.

The bathroom ceiling glistened as a peaceful sea of blue sky above them. Their faces shared the mirror and they were smiling. She was looking over his shoulder as he shaved. He had one free hand to pat her thigh with. There! All done scraping my face for another day," he said.

"Do you think the honeymoon is over now that we share our morning ablutions?" she asked with mock gravity.

"What are ablutions?" he returned.

"Brushing teeth, combing hair, pissing, showering, shitting, and shaving, and in general performing one's toilette." She grabbed his buttocks.

"Well, whatever ablutions are, and whether we share them or not, I am still madly in love with you. As a matter of fact, I am going to make you an omelette with white truffles for breakfast, my Princess of the Bathroom." He kissed her on the nose just like the leading man in a Hollywood movie.

"Oh, my dahlink, your lilps are as bitter-sweet as the music of Chopin!" she said in a Dietrich voice. "Let me kiss you endlessly," she laughed and tickled him under his third arm.

He dragged her into the shower with him and began to soap her breasts and navel and pubes all at once. She, of course, giggled, and, mostly because it tickled, since after several months of uninterrupted and passionate love making, there was absolutely no reason for her to feel shy.

It was not his third hand that pushed the elevator button. He still liked to keep his extra arm covered by his suit jacket when he was out and about and not at home or working at the bar. It was easier not to be stared at or to catch strangers doing double-takes as they passed him on the side-walk.

He had worked in the hotel bar for six months after taking over her job there. She had not wanted to stop working, but he had convinced her that she ought to begin taking classes in the evening at the local university. In the daytime, she stayed at home reading and studying and trying to write. She'd begun seven novels—all of them advanced by four or five chapters and none of them completed, but at least she had begun to try to write and she was happy about that.

Because *she* was happy, he was happy too.

After about four months of three-handed bar tending at the hotel, the owner, Abe Doyle, rented a mid-town bar, an exclusive place that changed its name to "The Third Arm" just to accommodate him, and to make him an attraction. An attraction he was!   In two months he'd earned almost two thousand dollars in tips alone. He worked from five in the evening to midnight, Tuesday through Saturday, and the place was always crowded. The customers came as much to watch him hustle drinks as to drink, his three hands flying before him, clinking glasses, tipping bottles, shaking cocktails, slicing limes and lemons with glorious speed and dexterity.

At first he had liked it, but during the last few weeks, he had begun to feel as though he had never really left the circus. If it wasn't for the fact that she was at home waiting for him, and if he did not love her so desperately and want so desperately to please her, he would quit. He knew it.

What he had really wanted was to be normal and anonymous. He had wanted to flow through the life of the city like the traffic in its streets. He had wanted to be hum-drum, to belong, to see how normal people live their two-handed, two-armed lives.

He had tried, at first, to work in the hotel bar with only two arms showing. He had even strapped his third arm down to his side, but it grew numb, made him feel claustrophobic, break out in a cold sweat, and nearly faint. When she explained his secret to Abe Doyle, who was her old boss, Doyle convinced him to work the bar three-handed. The short and squat Doyle was a keen business man with an eye for capitalizing wherever he could.

"My God, man," Abe Doyle had said. "You're a barkeeper's dream—a three-handed tender. You'll be superb that way. It'll be great for business!" Doyle's mouth fairly watered at the thought of the profits.

He was superb *that way* and it was great for business; and now he had an exclusive place named after him, a share in the profits, the tips rolling in; and she was in school and writing. Soon he would be able to buy the food and luxuries, save and invest money, and let her stay home, write, and go to school just as she had always wanted to.

As time passed they forgot how lonely they had been before they found each other. So content were they with each other's company and passionate affection that they never spent a day apart and foolishly forgot the necessities of solitude and a time away in which to refresh the solitary knowledge of their complete empathy.

"Sometimes I feel as though I have climbed into your skin and become you. When we make love and are as close as we are now, I can feel the responses of your nerves as if they were my own. It's incredible," she told him some months after they had been living as one.

"Do you realize how often you read my mind," he offered in return. "I'll be sitting there thinking something and you will say it. Often, I've had an itch behind my ear or in the center of my back and before I can reach to scratch it, you are scratching it for me."

"Remember the other day after work when you had a headache and I got one too and then when we massaged each other's temples it disappeared?"

"Yes."

"Well, I remember now, all that day in class as

I was trying to listen to the professors, I kept feeling as if I were in the bar working. I closed my eyes and saw your hands moving in front ot me pouring drinks. It was the strangest thing. As though I were you and seeing out of your eyes," she told him.

"I never believed it could be possible to love someone as much as I love you," he almost wept the words. She kissed his eyes.

They slept in each other's arms, comfortably, warmly, all through the night, feeling a contentment beyond all consciousness or words, loving each other's being more than their own.

It was Friday evening. A taxi carried her through wet streets. Sounds of engines and wheels sung around her. She was returning from a class in the early American novel. She held a paper-covered edition of Hawthorne's *Scarlet Letter* on her lap. She thought of Hawthorne's heroine, Hester Prynne, forced by a Puritan community to wear a red letter "A" on her breast for adultery. She thought of all the johns with wedding rings on their fingers who came to her during her two years of "turning tricks." Irony made her laugh a little out loud.

"If I wore a red "A" on my sweater, people would think it stood for the big apple, or that my name was Abigail or Alice, or that I like Op Art designs. I should get Emilio Pucci, or Peter Max, to make me a nice black Puritan blouse with a big day-glow red "A" on the front of it," she laughed to herself.

"What's so funny, Lady?" the cab driver said, thinking she had laughed at his nearly skidding into the car ahead as he came to a halt in front of "The Third Arm."

"Not you," she answered glibly, handing him a nice-sized tip along with her fare.

She liked to stop off for dinner and a drink on her way home after classes and he liked her to. It gave them both a sense of security to see each other early in the evening, before she went home to read and study and write and he finished out the night's work.

As she entered through the glass revolving doors and potted plants, she realized that she couldn't see the bar. It was completely crowded out of view by a sea of people. She wedged her way through the crowd. Living in the city had made her naturally apprehensive. She was afraid that something awful had happened—an accident or a murder. There was a policeman standing not far from the doors. "What's the matter; what's going on?" she asked, with apparent agitation.

"Nothin'," the policeman answered casually. "Just too much publicity for the size of this joint. That guy with three arms is workin' the bar, really puttin on a show, flippin' lemons in the air, shakin' up cocktails, tossin' bottles around! Everybody's waitin' to buy a drink just to see how fast he'll make it and what fancy tricks he'll do. This place is like a three-ring circus, Lady. If you really want a drink, you'd better go across the street..."

She was relieved for a moment from the ominous feeling that the overcrowded bar had produced in her, but, on second thought, she became a little terrified. She pushed ahead through the crowd, ducking under elbows to reach the mahogany counter. Finally, she managed a clear view. There he stood under the pink and yellow lights, his arms and hands flying before him. An olive was tossed into the air with one hand and caught in a martini glass with another while his third poured a second drink, and so on.

He was smiling, aware of all the eyes watching

him, but she knew him too well to believe in the smile. She saw the distress behind his eyes as he caught her eyes watching him. She saw his smile flicker and dim.

When he had arrived at work that evening, he had found the newspaper spread open on the bar and a photograph of himself, three hands gingerly mixing drinks, smiling up at him. The caption read: "Phenomenal mid-town bar tender at the busy 'Third Arm' displays super-human dexterity to dazzle his customers."

It was as if the almost-forgotten voice of the circus barker had dissolved into print, to resound again in his mind as he read the caption.

He decided to say nothing to his fellow barkeeper, Abe. He didn't want to offend or upset Abe with the anger that might fizzle up and pop uncorked from him. He knew that his partner-in-business would be thrilled about the publicity. It was better than any ad they might have purchased and it would make Abe happy.

Abe's face beamed as he greeted him. "How da ya like that article? Great, huh? Boy, that oughta bring'em flyin' in."

"Yes," he answered. "Great." He didn't want to spoil Abe Doyle's joy. He'd just begun to know the feeling of joy and he was, without really knowing it, sensitive to the aesthetic of it. He smiled falsely, nodded, and donned his bright blue bartending jacket. He was glad that somehow he had been the cause of Abe's beaming face, his pleasure and satisfaction. Behind that gladness an old anxiety, began to grope its way into him again, to knot his throat and stomach—an anxiety which floated in him like cold air beneath his warm happiness. With her, he felt the pure contentment he had known as a boy, when he had pleased his now dead parents by learning to juggle, play the piano, and display a dexterity which lead him to become a circus attraction, a performer capable of earning a sure living.

As the evening progressed, people began to pile in, as quickly as they might have piled into a circus tent. They grinned and leered and stretched their necks and shoved each other aside to order drinks: a double martini, a gin and tonic, a vodka Collins, a bourbon and water, scotch and soda, Bloody Marys, Side Cars, Rob Boys, Brandy Alexanders, Pink Ladies, Singapore Slings, Champagne Spritzers, Boiler Makers, Chartreuse, Creme de menthe on the rocks, Screw Drivers, Daiquiris.

"Heah, do you know what a *Dikery* on ice is?" one fat man asked him. "It's a factory at the North Pole where they manufacture lesbians." The man continued loudly, with great delight at himself, laughing and drooling a little into his Daiquiri.

Was it his imagination, or were they all drooling a little into their drinks? His hands worked furiously, mindlessly, gaining speed all the while, moving faster and faster. He was performing as well as he had ever performed. Just as they had in the circus, their eyes stared at him in fascination, and followed his hands as they might follow a glowing light swirling in darkness. He saw arcs of light sparkle from his working hands, glitter from glasses and the clear bronze and yellow liquids poured into them, glisten from wet rinds of limes, lemons, and sleek skins of cocktail onions, shine from silver mixing spoons and cocktail shakers, play through moving prisms of glass bottles. He created a dance of light before his own eyes. It soothed his mind, numbed it, shut him off from himself, made his hands and body separate from his thoughts and feelings.

Their eyes did not see him as human, but as

object, as phenomenon, as dazzling freak. He knew it and he locked the thought away in the cash register, ringing up sales, pocketing tips, listening to the music of clicking and clinking glasses, register bells, slap of change on counter, rustle of dollar bills, tingle of coins, sloshing and pouring of liquor, incessant din of voices jabbering and continuously ordering drink after drink. He had hypnotized himself into a kind of stupor that floated over his anxiety and wedged itself in his smile. He wore that stuperous smile absently until the moment he looked up and her face focused in out of a glob of glaring faces.

His eyes met hers exactly. He saw in them a kind of camouflaged revulsion, a sudden terror like that which he had seen the first night she had discovered his third hand reaching out from under his jacket to rescue her blue tablecloth from a tipping cup of coffee.

At the instant their eyes met, his hand slipped; a bottle crashed to the counter, splintering glass in all directions, splattering liquor onto the lap of a woman perched on the stool in front of him, holding her Pink Lady to her lips. "Goddamnit," shrieked the woman and the crowd laughed and gaffawed with one huge throated mouth.

In the next instant, his arms stopped flying before him and fell to his sides. As she dropped her gaze to the floor, his smile fell from his face.

She turned and wildly pushed her way through a blinding haze of laughing people, potted palms, police uniforms, and glass doorways. The cold outdoor air stung her face. She was worried. He had seen her turn and run from his gaze, but she couldn't make herself go back. He had caught her looking at him as though he were quite separate from herself—a strange thing, an object, a phenomenon, a freak.

It was not because he had dropped the bottle that she turned and ran. She knew that her face had blended, for a moment, with the face of the crowd and that he had read her mind, and discovered what was there: "He only loves me because he can't get someone better, I'm the only normal woman who ever responded to him. If he didn't have three arms, if he weren't a freak, he wouldn't want an ex-prostitute." These thoughts came to her in a wordless jumble as she walked quickly and determinedly along the pavement toward home.

He entered a dark hallway. It was peculiar because she always left the hall light on for him. Maybe the bulb had burned out.

Her voice came out of the darkness: "I'm here," she said flatly, "in the living room."

He walked in and snapped on the light. Her eyes blinked. She was sitting up upright on the sofa, her hands limp in her lap. She was dressed just as she had been earlier in the evening. She had not changed into any of the lacey negligees or night gowns he had bought for her during the past few months.

"It was a long and awful night," he said.

"I know," she said. "I'm sorry I made you drop that bottle."

"You didn't. It happens to the best of us freaks now and then," he added sarcastically.

"Well, the honeymoon *is* over. I just turned a trick. If you're still a freak, I'm still a whore too! That makes us just as even as we've always been."

"You what?"

"You heard me. I just turned a trick. I just brought a john up here with me, a cab driver. There's the money he left." She pointed to a crumple of bills lying on the other end of the sofa. "There!"

His legs became a gelatinous mass. He sank into the chair behind him. "You had a man up here?" He tried to realize what she had told him. "Why? Why? Not for money; we've got plenty of money. Why?"

"Because, I'm a whore, a prostitute, a woman who sells her body because there is no other kind of love but the kind you buy. One thing in exchange for another! You were working in that circus tonight to buy me; weren't you? You buy me because you can't get someone better, because you're a freak. We are not Romeo and Juliet, or Tristan and Isolde, or Elmira Madigan and Stephan, or even Doris Day and Rock Hudson. We are just a young whore and a middle-aged freak who need each other because we didn't find anyone else, or have anything better. You wouldn't love me if you didn't have three arms. I'm not beautiful. You tell me that to make me come, and you make me come because you know how to work my body with your three adept hands. The johns I picked up always treated me like an object. They didn't try to make me enjoy myself. I've been sitting here thinking. I realize that without the romantic haze of the past two years, without any lies covering and coating us, I am just a whore who will never be a writer, and you are a freak who will never really get out of the circus. What we have is not shining love. It's just drab desperate need." She said this all very flatly, never moving her eyes or her limp hands which lay in her lap like two dead birds upended.

They had lived together for two short years as new lovers do: talking all the talk that lovers talk from their warm pillows, sharing their pasts, dreams, hopes and desperations. They had wept confessions into each other's ears, sighed vows into each others eyes, and offered embrace, sweat to sweat, come to come, dream to dream. They had grown to know each other's fears and foibles, but all that had transpired between them, before this moment, had happened as if under water, as if photographed by a glycerine-coated lens, not rationally, but emotionally their imperfections had ceased to exist. They had become dreamers in a dream of love, characters in a love story viewed by the invisible third eyes in each of their heads.

With her speech, the screen became flooded with darkness; the third eyes in their heads blinked shut; the underwater swimmers surfaced; the glycerine was washed from the lens; they awoke and found themselves sitting across from each other in a blue living room in a glaring white light. He was staring at the pimple on her cheek; she was looking at the freckle on his nose.

She did not know what made her need to say to him what she had just said. Actually, she still wanted him, needed him, "loved" him, and yet, she had been driven to deliver her speech.

When she finished, he rose from his chair and came toward her. He pulled her up from the couch by her shoulders—not roughly, but firmly. He looked into her eyes as if searching for something there. His own eyes were wet and sharp with rage and bafflement. Pain pinched little wrinkles into the corners around them. He looked into her eyes and she stared back at him.

"I don't understand," he said, "I don't understand."

Her eyes fell from his penetrating gaze and he let go of her shoulders. He turned and walked out of the blue room, down the little hall, and exited, quietly closing the door behind him.

It was not until she had stood in the silence of

the room for a full three minutes that the tears began to burn her eyes and run down her cheeks. Then she collapsed in a sheer agony of loneliness on the sofa.

She had known such moments of perfection with him. It had been too good for her to bear. She did not love herself enough to take it. The intrusion of one sharp moment of revelation had compelled her to destroy it.

He walked the streets for hours. Then he ran through the city park until his lungs ached and his heart beat as though it would burst from his chest.

Finally, he found himself in a deserted shopping area. He peered through glass at the eery faces of mannequins with their perfectly arranged clothing and stiff flawless hair-dos. The thought that window dummies are like circus freaks, turned to plaster, crossed his mind. One mannequin, a blond dressed in a blue negligee, smiled weirdly at him. As he stared, her smile broadened to a grimace at the sight of him. He crossed the street. Sweat bubbled on his brow and ran into his eyes. The street lamps blurred. He collapsed against the window of a sporting goods store. There was a display of camping equipment neatly arranged before him. His eyes rested on theshiny steel blade of an ax which lay next to a plastic log in some fake bright green grass. The sight of the ax frightened him and sobered him at once. He tried to go on. He couldn't. His third arm seemed to weigh him down. It hung heavily at his side. He thought he would topple from its weight. At last, he collapsed at the curb, grabbing the metal-meshed litter basket before him. For a moment, he lay there, half on top of the over-turned basket, his face hanging into the debris of its spilled contents. When he pulled himself up a little he saw before him on the sidewalk, his own newspaper photograph, wrinkled with a mashed apple-core and a cigarette butt stuck to it. Again he read the caption: "Phenomenal mid-town bar tender at the busy Third Arm displays super-human dexterity to dazzle his customers."

As he pulled himself up from the litter basket, his three hands lifted it upright. On a sudden impulse, he swung around, the basket still in his arms. The sporting goods store stood before him. The mannequin with the blue negligee leered at him from the adjacent corner. He lifted and hurled the metal basket through the window of the sporting goods store. The glass cracked, splintered and fell tinkling to the sidewalk. Something in him exploded with the sound of cracking glass. His third hand grabbed the ax and he was off and running with a new burst of energy. He heard a burglar alarm screaming behind him. He ran faster down an alley, through another, toward the edge of town and the river. Two arms churned at his sides. The third clutched the ax to his chest.

He stood under the shadows of a bridge. White lights played in the rippling water. He shivered from the cold early morning air. Above the city skyline, the sky had turned a deep blue color just before dawn. He finished his last cigarette and threw it in the water. It became a tiny white speck, then disappeared from view. He knelt on one knee and stretched his third arm out along the jutting edge of a concrete piling. With a yank, he tore his third shirt sleeve from its shoulder seam and slid it from his third arm. The arm looked pale against the gray stone of the piling. He stretched it out and lifted the ax in his left hand. He knew it would take the strongest, most concentrated blow he could summon.

He lifted the ax high and let its clean sharp steel blade fall with all the might of pain within him.

It lay on the piling before him as he jerked and stood, stiffened up by the sudden pain, dizzied by an unbearable agony. He grabbed up the dead arm. At last, it was a thing separate from himself, its flesh weight strange in his hands. In a state of shock, not thinking, he hurled the thing, like a baseball bat, into the water ahead. As he threw it, blood whipped from it, splattering the piling and his face. He watched it float slowly down and away, staining the water, with a thin stream of dark blood trailing from it, just as he fainted...

He floated through water, free, swimming in the river. Women swam around him crying for help. He was trying to save them, but there were too many of them to rescue all at once. Each time he rescued one and carried her to the bank, three or four more appeared in the water, screaming for help. Cream-Puff, the circus fat lady, was drowning beside him. He grabbed for her, but busy eating rocks, she sank like an anchor pulling him down into the water.

As he went under, everything turned red. He sank to the bottom of a crimson world where he found her, looking like a mannequin with blond stiff hair, wearing a blue negligee, sprawled on a rock among the weeds. She told him that she had drowned from too much sex without love, but that she did not believe in love anyway. She told him they would be better off at the bottom of the river where they would eventually float out to sea together. No one else would find them to hurt them. They could pretend they were in love forever. He would never have to work in the circus again. She said that she liked him just the way he was, with all three of his hands touching her, working her body like a spaceship. He wanted to put his arms around her, but found they were gone. Then, he realized that the bleeding stumps of his arms were what was coloring the water red. "Darling, never mind," she said, "never mind. I'm here now. Everything will be all right."

"But, my arms, my arms, my arms!" He screamed and opened his eyes.

Her face was the face of a mannequin smiling down at him. "You'll be all right now," she said.

He turned his head toward the window. It was daylight outside. He tried to sit up in bed. A nurse appeared at the bedside and spoke to him. "Don't try to move yet! Just lie still. Your wife will stay here with you for awhile."

"My wife?" he asked, not understanding because he didn't really have a wife.

"I'm right here, darling." she said, her face surrounded by its halo of short blond curls focused into view again. "Lie still. Don't try to move yet." Her hand was on his forehead.

The nurse left the room.

"I'm sorry! I'm sorry!" she whispered weeping. "Forgive me, please. Somehow, you must forgive me."

He said nothing. Her hand felt heavy and rough on his forehead. He turned away from it. "Forgive you for what?" he asked. "There's nothing to forgive. Everything you said was true."

"No," she wept. "No, it wasn't."

"It was the way you saw it," he said. "It wasn't the way I saw it, but I wasn't seeing too clearly."

"Yes, yes you were! You were seeing more clearly than I," she answered, desperately trying to be convincing.

There was a long silence.

"The doctor says you'll be out of here in another week or two. You lost a lot of blood, but you'll be okay. You had three transfusions. The surgeon says he patched you up good as new. With a little plastic surgery, he says you will hardly have a scar where your arm used to be." She smiled reassuringly.

"No scar?" he said, and he laughed ironically. "No scar."

During his convalesence, she was more tender and loving than she had ever been, but it didn't seem to matter to him. He still loved her, but she could have stood on her head and spit nickels for love of him and it wouldn't have mattered.

He appreciated her attentions and was kind, civil and polite. He thanked her for every cup of tea or bowl of soup she served him in bed, but it didn't matter and she sensed it didn't. After three weeks of nursing him at home and putting up with his civility, she began to have nightmares about his leaving her. She awoke one night in a sweat and turned over to find him gone from the bed. She jumped up and rushed into the hall. He was standing in the dark living room, silhouetted against the window, looking out. She went to him and stood close behind him and put her arms gently around him and rubbed his stomach. "Can't sleep?" she asked. "Talk to me. Tell me. What is it?" She spoke tenderly. "You haven't forgiven me. I know it and I don't blame you..."

"Yes, I've forgiven you." he said. "But, there really isn't anything to forgive, and it doesn't matter."

She slid his pajama bottoms down, and kissing him to convey all the real ardency she felt, she touched him tenderly with longing. He drew away from her touch as he never had before and moved to look out of the window at the street below. It was the first time her touch had ever failed to excite him and she felt helplessly devoid, all of a sudden, of any power to tempt him to her will.

"...I love you," she said. "Please forgive me. I need your forgiveness. I know that dreams can only be lived if we promise to dream the same dream together. Please forgive me." She went up behind him and held him closely, resting her head on his back, but he did not turn to her.

"I forgive you, but it doesn't matter," he spoke quietly without anger.

"Why doesn't it matter?"

"I don't know. I can't help it. I've thought about it a lot. I think I understand. Look at me!" He opened his pajama tops. "I'm a normal, ordinary man." He pulled the bandage off his side. "See, only these two red scars, here and here, and the doctor says they'll fade and become even less deep after awhile. They might nearly disappear. Don't you see? I don't need to be loved by you, or anyone now. I don't feel the way I used to. I look around me and nothing's the same as it was. The room looks faded and it used to look so bright and blue. The flowers you bring in don't smell the way they used to. Your face is not as fascinating as it used to be to me, but you haven't changed. It's me! I don't see things the way I used to, or feel them the way I used to. I feel numb. Nothing's as bright, as wonderful, as lovely or mysterious as it used to be. I'm ordinary and normal. Maybe this is what it's like to feel ordinary and normal like everybody else. No one will ever look at me as a freak or make me feel like a freak again. I wish I could talk as poetically as you can sometimes so I could tell you what I mean....It's as if taking away what made me different has taken away my spirit to strive for life...to live...to love...as if I chopped out my soul when I chopped off my extra arm...as if what was imperfect or freakish about me made me feel or see things more deeply. It's as if I left my soul at the bottom of the river with my arm." He collapsed onto the sofa. His pajama bottoms still down around his thighs, his soft genitals dangling from him, making him look lost and vulnerable.

He sat there quietly with his head down and then spoke again, not looking at her. "You made me see things as they really were...'our drab desparate need,' you said....Well, I don't feel any desperation anymore. I'll never work in the circus again. I'll never entertain people as I did. No one will stare at me as if I wasn't human again, but I won't amaze people with my skill either. I don't know what to say to you except that I don't believe in romance anymore. I don't believe in...in..."

"In love?" she said sadly, finishing his sentence with a question. She had been meaning to tell him about what really occurred the night she was forced to turn a trick. She wanted to tell him how she hadn't chose to but was forced, but somehow she felt very guilty about it, as if it was her fault, in any case, because of her past. His words took all desire to explain out of her. She felt his depression and took the guilt for it into her heart and couldn't speak. "I only believed in it because you taught me to," she said, feeling properly rejected by him. I believed in it because of the way your hands touched me, conveying love. You taught me to touch you like that and now you don't want me to.

She awoke and rolled over. The bed was strangely empty. She opened her puffed and swollen eyes. Sun streaked across her chest. She dragged her feet from the bed to the floor. It was true. He had gone. It wasn't just a bad dream this time. There was the checkbook on the night table where he'd left it the evening before. When she opened the closet to get her robe, she was struck by its emptiness on the side where his suits had hung. She had watched him pack the night before. A few of his white shirts, pushed to one side, still drooped from their hangers. Noticing that her arms felt like lead, she pulled a shirt from its hanger and held it up in front of her. Three sleeves drooped from it. She spread it out on the bed, fanning its three sleeves out from its sides, and buried her face in the cloth smell. She lay down on top of it, breathing it in. It smelled like him: an aroma she had come to associate with sexual desire. She remembered the first night with him, how patiently his three hands massaged her, gently, incessantly, to make her feel an ecstasy she had never known, a release of demons from her flesh.

She knew that she would never be able to turn a trick again. She was cured forever of not believing in love. She knew that it was not because she had been a whore that he had left her. It was no longer important to her that she had been one. At least, that had stopped troubling her and she knew it would never trouble her again.

The room was hot and dry. She got up and pushed the window open. Cool early morning air made her shiver. She took his shirt from the bed and dried her burning eyes on it, then slipped her arms into it and wrapped it around herself. She looked into the bureau mirror, wet her finger and rubbed the smudges of mascara from under her red eyes. A third sleeve dangled under her right armpit. She wrapped it around her breasts.

"I've got to leave!" he had said. "I don't know exactly where. I'll start by flying to London tonight. I'll write as soon as I can bring myself to. I don't know if I'll be back. I'm leaving you half of our savings, half of all that was left after hospital bills. Here's the checkbook! I've put my half into travelers'checks. I'm sorry that I can't stay. I can't feel anything. Maybe I'll learn to again. It's not that I'm blaming you. It's just the way it is. I wish I could stay and make you happy again, but I can't. You know it's got nothing at all to do with your past, because that never mattered to me."

She looked up and thought she saw his face in the mirror in place of her own. It frightened her. "It's this shirt," she told herself.

She went into the bathroom. "I think there are still some of those sleeping pills he was taking when he first came home from the hospital," she thought. She opened the medicine chest and found the yellow pills on the top shelf. "I'll take one. I can't stand being awake. I don't want to think. My head will split open."

She swallowed one of the pills with a glass of water and returned to the bedroom. As she climbed back into bed with the shirt wrapped around her, she noticed that her side ached a little just below her right armpit. She rubbed it and thought she felt a swelling and then drifted into sleep.

Something clutched her throat. She was suffocating. In terror, she opened her eyes on the darkness of the room and tried to sit up in bed, but a heavy weight rested on her neck. She moved her right hand to her throat, but her other hand was already there clutching it. She tried to scream but couldn't. She struggled upright and reached for the light switch. As her left hand flicked it on, she realized that there were still two hands at her throats She screamed and then she saw it, coming from the sleeve under her right armpit. She held it up in front of her face. It seemed to view her with an eyeless gaze. She thought she would faint from looking at it. She blinked her eyes. It was still there. She moved her fingers and it moved its. She took it in her other hands. It resembled exactly, in every detail, her right hand. Even the nails were painted with the same clear pink polish she always wore. She thought she must be dreaming as it helped her right hand throw the covers back. She ran through the hall to the bathroom. It flicked on the light for her. She stubbed her toe on the threshold and her toe throbbed with the pain. Perhaps she wasn't dreaming. It turned on the water and helped her other two hands splash cold water into her face. She shook her head; she blinked her eyes. Her three hands slapped and pinched her cheeks. She was awake ....

The word nocturnal brings emissions of darkness from the listening eyes of birds. All the answers are in the light and the sun from which it evolves in our sleepless turnings. We never truly sleep because the real meanings are in the schizophrenia of dreams that flash in light beneath our eyelids. There is an essence of light in the fullness of a penis or a tongue and one of darkness in the hollow of a vagina or a mouth and an attraction between like that of land and water, once divided, but both essential to life. Even in the driest cactus there is a vein of water that brings life to the sterile sand. Love with the body is a primal sacrament of light and light and life are one substance in schizophrenia, in dreams, and in love, as in all the traditions of myth and poetic imagery. A fullness in the hollow of dreams informs the body that it is to love with as the hands are to be with. The body is light and the whole body is a phallus to the darkness. Where the darkness copulates with the light, the world is born again in the dawn of every morning to the sounds of birds singing songs of refracted irridescence as if discovering the turnings of the day upon the night as one body pours light into the darkness of another, pours hard full lit meanings into the dark wet hollows of dreams.

DANIELA GIOSEFFI, poet, novelist, editor, critic, multi-media performer—achieved critical acclaim for her first book of poems, *Eggs in the Lake* [Boa Editions, 1979.] Nona Balakian, former reviewer for *The New York Times*, wrote of the book: "One of the finest new poets around. Her work overflows with poetic vision. Nothing is ever pretentious or done for effect." Her most recent book of poetry is *Word Wounds and Water Flowers* [VIA Folios, 1995]. Gioseffi's novel, *The Great American Belly*, was published by Doubleday & Dell in 1979. Larry McMurtry, in *The Washington Post*, called the novel: "Engaging, filled with energy ...irresistible writing." Her book, *On Prejudice: A Global Perspective* [Doubleday/Anchor, 1993] won an award from The Ploughshares Fund World Peace Foundation.

Gioseffi was a featured speaker on world peace and disarmament at the Barcelona International Bookfair, 1990, and at the Miami International Bookfair, 1991, where she was presented with an American Book Award for her edited and annotated, international compendium *Women on War* [Simon & Schuster/Touchstone,1988]. Carl Sagan called it: "A book of searing analyses and cries f rom the heart on the madness of war."

Gioseffi's poetic plays, "The Sea Hag in the Cave of Sleep" and "Daffodil Dollars" have been produced Off-Broadway. She won PEN's 1990 Short Fiction Award for "Daffodil Dollars." The piece also aired on National Public Radio's "The Sound of Words." Her poems, stories, criticism, essays and interviews have appeared in leading periodicals, such as *The Paris Review, Ms., The Nation, Antaeus, Choice, The American Book Review*, and *The New York Times*.

The author began her career as a journalist in Selma,

Alabama in 1961, during the early days of the civil rights movement, and helped to integrate Southern television. She has worked in the Gandhian world peace and justice movement ever since. She lived for nearly thirty years in New York City before settling back in her home state of New Jersey. Through the 1980's, Gioseffi served on the nominating committee for The Olive Branch Book Awards of the Writers and Publishers Alliance. Apart from her literary endeavors, she has worked as a professional actress, dancer, and singer.

GLOUCESTER COUNTY LIBRARY

3 2928 00 152 9605

9/97

DATE DUE

DEMCO 38-296